Erik Satie

En art, il faut croire avant d'y aller voir.

Léon-Paul Fargue.

The MIT Press
Massachusetts Institute of Technology
Cambridge, Massachusetts, and London, England

Erik Satie

Pierre–Daniel Templier

Translation by
Elena L. French and David S. French

The Satie discography has been supplied by Jeffrey Cobb

Originally published in French, under the same title, by Presses Universitaires de France

Set in Linofilm Palatino
Printed and bound in the United States of America by
The Riverside Press, Inc.

Library of Congress catalog card number: 69–12760

To Darius Milhaud

Contents

List of Illustrations   ix

1 His Life   1

Honfleur   1
His family   2
His childhood   3
Music   7
Arcueil   22
Recognition   31
Parade   36
Socrate and its disciples   41
The musique d'ameublement   45
Mercure and Relâche   49

2 The Man   55

3 His Works   75

Prior to the Schola Cantorum   75
Fugues and wit   80
Parade   86
Socrate   91
After Socrate   102
Mercure   104
Relâche   108

4 En Plus   113

Discography   117

viii

I wish to thank M. Conrad Satie, without whose assistance this book could never have been written—or illustrated. With a kindness and trust that I will never forget, he allowed me to examine all the precious documents which he has kept. Thanks are also due to M. Darius Milhaud, M. Roger Désormière, M. Pierre Bertin, and M. Rolf de Maré, who kindly let me have the manuscripts, drawings, and letters which were in their possession, as well as to the publishers of Satie's works (Rouart Lerolle et Cie, La Sirène, Universal Edition), who allowed me to consult Satie's orchestral scores.

Pierre-Daniel Templier

List of Illustrations

1. Erik Satie's father.
2. Erik Satie's mother.
3. Birth announcement of Erik Satie.
4. Erik Satie as a child.
5. Erik Satie as a child.
6. Olga Satie.
7. Erik Satie's birth house in Honfleur. (Photograph by Mulot, Honfleur.)
8. Conrad Satie.
9. Sanguine sketch dated 1890, inscribed "To my Friend Erik Satie."
10. Portrait of Satie, about 1892.
11. Rent receipt, rue Cortot.
12. Rue Cortot, Montmartre. The house in which Satie lived (No. 6) is in the center.
13. Erik Satie, between 1895 and 1900.
14. Erik Satie, "the grey velvet gentleman," 1895.
15. Erik Satie, between 1895 and 1900.
16. Erik Satie with Claude Debussy, about 1910.
17. Erik Satie, about 1911.
18. At Claude Debussy's house, about 1910.
19. Photograph found among Satie's effects (taken before 1900).
20. Photograph found among Satie's effects (taken before 1900).
21. No. 29, rue Cauchy at Arcueil. The window of Satie's room is on the third floor.
22. No. 29, rue Cauchy at Arcueil.
23. Satie in Montmartre, between 1900 and 1905.
24. Erik Satie, photographed by Man Ray on February 15, 1922.
25. Erik Satie.
26. Erik Satie.
27. Erik Satie.

28. Erik Satie and Pierre Bertin at Fontainebleau.
29. Erik Satie, "the grey velvet gentleman," 1895.
30. Medallion for the book cover on the libretto of "Uspud." Designed by Suzanne Valadon.
31. Inscription by Erik Satie.
32. Sketch of Suzanne Valadon, by Erik Satie.
33. Sketch by Erik Satie, about 1895.
34. Sketch by Erik Satie, about 1895.
35. Sketch by Erik Satie, about 1895.
36. Organization list of the Metropolitan Church of Art of Jesus the Conductor. Black and red. Satie's handwriting.
37. Dedication by Claude Debussy on a copy of Baudelaire's "Poèmes."
38. Calligraphic inscription in Erik Satie's handwriting.
39. Letter from Monsieur Dépaquit addressed to Erik Satie (on the verso of a letter by Satie).
40. Letter from Satie to his brother.
41. Ticket of admission to a wine party given in honor of Satie's nomination to the Academy.
42. The Administrative Council of the *Laic Patronage* in Arceuil (1909).
43. Letter from Satie to his brother, on the occasion of the first concert of the Société Musicale Indépendante (S.M.I.), January 14, 1911.
44. Notes found among Satie's effects.
45. Self-portrait of Erik Satie.
46. Self-portrait of Erik Satie.
47. Laundry slip.
48. Letter to a friend, July 27, 1918.
49. Letter to a friend, July 27, 1918.
50. Sketches by Erik Satie, about 1920.
51. Inscriptions by Erik Satie, about 1920.
52. Sketches by Erik Satie, about 1920.
53. Designs and inscriptions by Erik Satie, about 1920.
54. Designs and inscriptions by Erik Satie, about 1920.
55. Designs and inscriptions by Erik Satie, about 1920.
56. Designs and inscriptions by Erik Satie, about 1920.
57. Political inscription by Erik Satie.
58. Letter addressed to L. L. Veyssière at the time of the split between the Socialist and Communist parties.
59. Postal card addressed to L. L. Veyssière. (Tulard is the name of a café in Arceuil.)
60. Satie and Cocteau. Drawing by Pablo Picasso.
61. Caricature of Satie, 1916.
62. Erik Satie, photograph by Man Ray, 1923–24.
63. First page of the autograph manuscript of the first Gymnopédie (1888).
64. Page from the manuscript of Geneviève de Brabant, about 1900. Found behind the piano.
65. Postal-card advertisement, with Satie's *Valse*.
66. Statement of account of the Society of Authors and composers, amounting to 76 centimes.

67. Test paper for the Schola Cantorum: analysis of a motet by Palestrina. Instructor's annotation: "Analysis very well begun; too bad it was not finished."
68. Test paper for the Schola Cantorum: analysis of Maurice Ravel's "Noël des Jouets."
69. Diploma from the Schola Cantorum for work in counterpoint.
70. Autograph page from Third *Valse*: "Le précieux dégoûté," 1914.
71. Two different versions of "Daphénéo" (1916). The second version is the final one; a third one is sketched in the same notebook.
72. Autograph page from "Parade": First Manager.
73. Decorations for "Parade" by Pablo Picasso.
74. Rough draft for lecture on the spirit of music.
75. Two pages of a notebook in which Satie copied the libretto of "Le Médecin malgré lui." Rhythmic patterns for the recitatives are given on the facing pages (1923).
76. Erik Satie, by Pablo Picasso. (*From: Revue Musicale.*)
77. Erik Satie, by Pablo Picasso. (*Galerie Rozenberg.*)
78. Erik Satie playing golf, with the sculptor Constantin Brancusi (1923).
79. Erik Satie on the roof terrace of the Théâtre des Champs-Elysées, during the filming of "Entr'acte." Shown are Borlin, Satie, and, in shirt sleeves, Picabia and René Clair.
80. Decoration and costumes for "Mercure," by Pablo Picasso. (*Photo Waléry.*)
81. Page from the rough draft for "Mercure," part 3.
82. Page from the program for the "Ballets Suédois," 1924. Design by Francis Picabia.
83. Musical outline for "Cinéma."
84. Stage design for "Relâche," by Francis Picabia, 1924. (*Photo Isabey.*)
85. Erik Satie about 1918.

Picture Credits

The following illustrations were kindly supplied by Conrad Satie: 3–6, 8, 9, 14–18, 31–35, 38, 40, 41, 44–46, 50–57, 74, 78.

Darius Milhaud furnished the following illustrations: 63, 67, 68, 71–73, 75, 81, 83.

The following illustrations are from the collection of Roger Désormière: 10, 11, 30, 37, 64, 66, 69.

Pierre Bertin supplied illustrations 25–28, 48, 49.

L. L. Veyssière supplied illustration 42.

Rolf de Maré supplied illustrations 79 and 82.

1

His Life

Honfleur

*Although our
information is incorrect,
we do not vouch for it.*
Erik Satie

Honfleur is a charming little town, descending in terraces along the side of the superb Colline de Grâce. A gentle and somewhat pale light lends an air of mystery to the old houses, tall and sad, mirrored in dark pools. "The poetic waters of the Seine and the turbulent waters of the Channel" mingle at the feet of the old city of sailors and fishermen, and the mists rising from them instill the "very polite and very friendly inhabitants" with a spirit that can be found nowhere else. A whimsical and peculiar spirit, made of happy opposites and absurd contrasts. Here people are gay, noisy, mischievous but with moments of melancholy gravity; they claim to be original yet are dreadfully bourgeois, dignified, and suspicious. The very bell-towers cross the squares to keep an eye on their churches. No one can tell, however, whether the natives of Honfleur laugh up their sleeves when they appear indignant and whether they are furious when they slap their thighs; the comical petty hatreds could very well be pretexts for making fun of one's neighbor or of oneself.

Honfleur is the birthplace of many famous men: we will only mention the two most characteristic ones, the humorist Alphonse Allais and Erik Satie.

The great-grandfather was a naval captain under the Empire. From his battles, from his victories over the English, he brought back trophies and a great hatred for the islanders. His son, Jules Satie, a ship broker, captain of the fire brigade, holder of the Légion d'honneur, was a person of standing, well known for his integrity and his intransigence. Intransigence is the main fault—or the great virtue—of the Saties.

Jules Satie married a girl of Alsatian origin (this Alsatian blood was not taken into account in the upbringing of the family musician) and had three children: Alfred, Adrien, and Marguerite. The two brothers had opposite personalities: Alfred was studious and obedient, his brother unruly. Boarders at the Collège d'Honfleur, they did not stay there for long; although Adrien did not continue his studies, Alfred was sent to the Collège at Lisieux where he obtained his baccalauréat. An excellent student, he became a close friend of his brilliant classmate Albert Sorel, also born in Honfleur.

The two brothers then left for England, where they stayed with a clergyman. By his pranks, Adrien, nicknamed "Sea-Bird," roused to indignation the faithful gathered in church for services. Having been forbidden to enter the church, he scandalized

The origins of the Satie family may go back far into the past. Yes. Beyond this I can affirm nothing—nor can I refute anything, for that matter. I believe, however, that this family did not belong to the nobility and that its members were good and modest laborers subject to serfdom.
Erik Satie

the town; confined to the cottage, he debauched the maids. After a second trip, this time to Norway, Jules Satie set up both his sons in business as ship brokers. "Sea-Bird" lacked enthusiasm for his work and proved to be deplorably original outside it, but his respect and his submission to his father's authority led him to continue the office. As for Alfred, he took his role very seriously.

Jane Leslie Anton, born in London of Scottish parents, lost her father at an early age. Her mother, who came from a simple family, served as lady's-maid to her wealthy sister who was married to a Mr. MacCombay, Anglican and pious. On a trip to Paris, Mr. MacCombay distributed moralistic pamphlets. His nephew's son would also distribute pamphlets, later, at the doors of concert halls. Jane Anton was sent to a boarding school in Honfleur. Alfred met her, they fell in love and were married. Members of the respectable Satie family, Catholic and anglophobe, and members of the dignified Anton family eyed each other silently and uncordially.

The newlyweds left for their honeymoon, Jane guiding her happy husband through the treasures of Scotland. On their return, they announced the forthcoming birth of a young Satie.

His childhood

I came to this world very young at a very old time.
Erik Satie

Erik Alfred Leslie came to "this earth, so earthly and so earthy," on May 17, 1866, at 9 in the morning. "Was I sent here to enjoy myself? to have a bit of fun? ... To forget the misery of another world which I can no

longer remember? Am I not intruding here?"
Comparing Satie to Sleeping Beauty, Cocteau claimed that French and English
fairies stood around the child's cradle. We
may add that the old witch also came and
said: "And my gift to you shall be judgment
so infallible that it will discourage you."

Erik's sister Olga was born in 1867,
and his brother Conrad in 1869. The three
children were baptized in the Anglican
faith: the Satie clan muttered! The young
family lived too close to the grandparents,
and the increasing strain in their relations
worried Alfred. At the end of the Franco-
Prussian war he sold his business and
moved with his family to Paris, where Jane
died in 1872.

Erik hardly knew his mother. This may
perhaps account for his tendency toward
solitary meditation and for the spirit of independence which would later characterize
him. The two little boys were left to the care
of their grandparents and rebaptized into
the Catholic religion. The Antons, dignified
as ever, bid farewell and left. At the age of
six, Erik was sent as a boarder to the Collège d'Honfleur where he remained until
1878. Following in his uncle "Sea-Bird's"
footsteps, he was not very obedient, and his
teachers had a low opinion of him.

After his wife's death, Alfred Satie
cultivated his studious tendencies and his
love for foreign languages. He traveled, spent
a year in Lübeck, a year in Milan. Returning
to Paris, he took courses at the Sorbonne and
at the Collège de France. On Sundays he
dined with Albert Sorel, Secretary General of

the Senate, at Versailles. Here he met very "proper" people, people who were or would later become members of the Académie française. His friend found him a job as a translator.

In Honfleur, young Eric grew up strong and healthy, surrounded by his grandfather, an old unbeliever, his grandmother, pious and high-minded, and his brother Conrad, thoughtful and obedient. He spent a lot of his time with his uncle "Sea-Bird," for whom he felt a singular attraction. This uncle was divided between his love for ships and his love for horses. He owned a splendidly painted carriage that no one dared enter for fear of ruining it, just like the famous staircase invented by Erik Satie. He would sit before his favorite horse, quietly smoking. He had a magnificent boat built for himself, "The Wave," all the more precious because it was useless; from time to time, the master would smoke a pipe on board his yacht but he seldom took it out to sea. On great occasions, he would leave the port, accompanied by a sailor with the Shakespearian name "Ass's Jawbone" sail around for a while and return. When touring theatrical troupes performed at Honfleur, he would take his nephew Erik along and smuggle him backstage. This immoral uncle left the brokerage business on his father's death, bought a bookstore, entrusted its management to an old saleslady, and devoted himself entirely to hippology and seamanship.

Erik took piano lessons from the organist of St. Catherine's church, Vinot, whose influence on the child was undoubtedly great. Vinot, who had studied under Niedermeyer, may have initiated him in the old Gregorian modes and plain song. Did the child show a natural gift? The period remains unmarked by any prodigious accomplishments.

In 1878 his grandmother died under strange circumstances, while swimming near the little beach at Honfleur. His grandfather became a convert and a faithful churchgoer. He carried to the services an unusual prayer book: "Les Harmonies de la Nature" by Bernardin de Saint-Pierre. After his first communion, Erik went to live with his father in Paris. It was the good life for him. Alfred Satie, bitterly disillusioned by formal pedagogy, gave his son complete freedom, while providing informal guidance, and took him out of school for good; but he took Erik with him to lectures and classes at the Collège de France. On Sundays Erik (or Crin-Crin, as he was called in the family) went with his father to Albert Sorel's home. Here Alfred had met a young girl, a piano teacher, whom he married in 1879, to Crin-Crin's distress. Unfortunately, Mademoiselle Barnetsche was accompanied by a cumbersome mother, and the presence of both a stepmother and a mother-in-law weighed heavily on young Erik.

The newly married couple shared a real passion for music. Madame Satie had studied under Alexandre Guilmant and Mathias. Hers was a very academic spirit. Satie's hatred for this spirit dates from this first contact with it.

Music
*All great artists are
amateurs.*
Erik Satie

Erik had come to love the piano which, "like money, pleases only those who touch it," and his parents decided to make him study seriously. Was he enthusiastic? He later claimed that he was forced into a musical career. It is true that his parents' proselytism had no limits. At the Rue de Constantinople, where the family lived, the concierge's daughter joined the Opéra-Comique. Full of admiration, or perhaps forced by his stepmother, Erik went to hear Guilmant at the Trinité and became an assiduous follower of the Trocadéro concerts. His father, wishing to complete Erik's education, found a Latin and Greek instructor for him. Monsieur Mallet, once a professor in a Jesuit school, owned a stationery store in the Rue de Rome. He had a daughter. By an ingenious exchange, Mademoiselle Mallet took piano lessons, while Crin-Crin learned—or rather did not learn—Latin. Monsieur Mallet would come to the Saties' apartment to give his lessons: the teacher and the pupil would retire to the living room; Erik had not learned his lesson. "Review, my friend," M. Mallet would say and immediately fall asleep. The young Latinist would neither move nor breathe until his teacher woke up. His progress was rather slow.

He did not do much better at the Conservatory, where he was sent in 1879. For the rest of his life he had bad memories of this "vast, uncomfortable, and rather ugly building; a sort of penitentiary with no beauty on the inside—nor on the outside, for that matter." Painstakingly he went through Descombes' and Lavignac's classes in elementary piano and solfeggio.

Erik spent a great deal of his time reading; this was a family vice. He read his father's favorite books: "Le Siècle de Louis XIV," novels by Dumas père and by Chavette. A little later he read Alphonse Karr, Méry, de Musset; he discovered Andersen, who was to remain a favorite for the rest of his life. The musicians he admired were all very respectable: above all Bach, to whose works Vinot and Guilmant had introduced him; then Chopin and Schumann. Already at this early age he made fun of grand opera and preferred Messager's musical comedies. In 1884 he entered Mathias's piano class and in 1885 Taudou's harmony class. Satie was to quote Taudou as insisting: "You really should devote yourself to the piano," while Mathias would rebut: "You really were made to compose." Did he compose prior to this period? His first work, published in 1887 but composed two years earlier, is marked Op. 62. But where was his sense of humor? The work consisted of a "Valse-ballet" and a "Fantaisie-Valse," both very sober, which appeared in a publication called "La Musique des Familles," a title that needs no comment:

We present today a charming waltz-fantasy for piano by Erik Satie. This composition is the work of a very young musician; its construction is elegant and its rhythm graceful and full of feeling. All the composer's works (?), of which we will mention three melodies, show a propensity for revery and a tendency to depart from the rigid laws of rhythmic symmetry.

These piano pieces were followed by three settings of poems by J.-P. Contamine de Latour who was at the time Satie's collaborator. De Latour, a young writer of Spanish origin, nicknamed "le Vieux Modeste" by Satie, coldly imitated Flaubert and Péladan. Though his plans were fantastic, his achievements were far less so. But what did that matter? He claimed to be related to Napoleon and was full of ideas. In 1889 he published five short stories, the first of which was dedicated to Erik Satie. They had met through young seamstresses whom they were courting.

The poems for which Satie composed melodies were not very good ones, but their gentleness suited well the young, shy, and nearsighted musician.

I have watched—like a dream—
   A cruel hoax,
All my happiness decline.
Instead of joyous hopes
   I suffer pain
   And heartache . . . .

"Les Anges," "Les Fleurs," "Sylvie," these were the titles of the songs published by Alfred Satie, Boulevard Magenta in Paris; "all rights reserved for all countries." Erik's father had tried his luck in different occupations but had never been successful. Together with the Barnetsche family he had opened a music school in the Rue de Turbigo; this was hardly a solid enterprise and the results were not encouraging. After Jules Satie's death, he had bought, with his father's savings, a stationery store in the Boulevard Magenta. Madame Barnetsche, Erik's old enemy, ran the store. Soon a music counter was added: Euterpe was ever present! Alfred had then abandoned the stationery store to become a music publisher. He published café-concert songs, his son's melodies, and some compositions by a young friend of Erik's, Charles Levadé. Gradually he lost all of his modest fortune.

Under the combined influences of Contamine de Latour, the books he read, and Gregorian music, Erik Satie lapsed into a naive and slightly mocking mysticism. He spoke endlessly of "his religion" and carefully followed its strict commandments. He affected a deep humility and his friends called him "Monsieur le Pauvre." He spent his days at Notre-Dame, where the semi-darkness is favorable to reveries, or else read with passion at the National Library the ponderous writings of Viollet le Duc on Gothic art. During this period he wrote four "Ogives," clumsy but charming testimonies of this passionate and naive period.

These melancholy crises left him little time for the Conservatory. He was anxious to be rid of this formal teaching. Had he not registered for Taudou's course in order to have the right to enlist in the army? On November 15, 1886, he left for Arras, full of enthusiasm, to join the 33d Infantry Regiment. However, he soon tired of this new life where instruction was as formal and boring as the teaching of deceptive cadences. To get out of the barracks he resorted to drastic methods. On a cold winter night, he stood out in the open, his chest bared. He came down with severe bronchitis and spent three peaceful months convalescing. He read

Flaubert's "Salammbô" over and over and
was thrilled by it; then "La Tentation de
Saint Antoine," which amused him and appealed to his imagination. He discovered
Péladan: doubtless, he enjoyed the writings
of the Sâr—"Le Vice suprême," "L'Andro-
gyne"—but he was certainly much more
attracted by the mysterious character of the
author himself, who brought back to life,
through the Rosicrucians, the secret societies
of the Middle Ages. During his convales-
cence, he began his delightful "Gymnopédies" which he claims were inspired by
"Salammbô." But they are infinitely purer
than Flaubert's evocations and seem to
represent very clearly, in music, Puvis de
Chavannes' paintings, which Satie loved.
During one of his leaves Satie went to see a
performance of "Le Roi malgré lui" by
Emmanuel Chabrier, presented by the
Opéra-Comique. Carried away by his enthusiasm for the composer's daring, Satie
left with Chabrier's doorman one of his
works, decorated with a superb dedication
—in red ink, of course. Good old Chabrier
did not deign to answer.

In September 1887 he wrote his three
exquisite "Sarabandes" which bear as
epigraph a verse by Contamine de Latour:

*The heavens opened all at once, and the cursed
fell . . . .*

The verse is outmoded but the music is not.
Released from military service in November,
he did not return to the Conservatory, nor
did he ever regret it. Montmartre attracted
him: he soon became a regular customer at
the "Chat-Noir" where he met his fellow

Honfleurais, Alphonse Allais. In becoming
friends, they did no more than continue
family traditions: the pharmacist Allais
had long known the Satie family. At the
"Chat-Noir," Erik soon became part of the
gay group comprised of Georges Auriol,
Maurice Donnay, Jouy, Rivière, Tinchant.
The following year, Rodolphe Salis took him
on as second pianist. Erik's physical appear-
ance began to change: he let his beard grow,
to conform with the ways of the "Chat-
Noir." He wore a top hat and a flowing
neckerchief. He also changed his way of life;
as a result of a love affair with a little maid
in his parents' house, he moved out and settled in a large room in the Rue Condorcet,
where he could be free and undisturbed. He
was greatly impressed by the exotic music
he heard at the 1889 Exhibition, particularly
that of Rumania. The influence of the Exhibition on the young musicians of that
period is well known. Satie's "Gnossiennes,"
written in 1890, are bathed in this curious
mixture of Orientalism and Gregorian mysticism.

"Monsieur le Pauvre" was not rich, but
he was still on good terms with his family.
Occasionally friends would invite him to
dinner and encourage him. Among these
was the musician Léopold Dauphin, whose
daughter had married Franc-Nohain. Léopold Dauphin once said, with some wit,
that the "Gymnopédies" seemed to have
been written by a savage with taste. Every
Sunday Erik dined with his brother Conrad,
who gave him endless encouragement
through their long and gentle philosophical

discussions. Conrad Satie was perhaps the only one who understood him completely even at that early stage.

The Rue Condorcet did not seem Bohemian enough to the young musician; he climbed the Rue des Martyrs and settled in a room in an old house at No. 6, rue Cortot. He furnished this room to his own taste: a bench, a table, a chest. Around 1890, he met Josephin Péladan, High Priest of both the Wagnerian cult and of the "Rose + Croix du Temple et du Graal," the Rosicrucian sect in France. Satie was not a Wagnerian but he was delighted to join the society and to become the musician-laureate of the Brotherhood.

In 1891 he composed the incidental music for "Le fils des étoiles," described by the author, Péladan, as a "wagnérie kaldéenne". The words were wholly subservient to Richard Wagner's esthetics while the music turned its back on it with disdain. Péladan had submitted the play unsuccessfully to the Comédie française. Claretie said to him: "Your play is something like literary music." Here is an example:

That which is above is like that which is below;
And that which is below
Is like that which is above to accomplish the miracles
of will.
Will rises from the earth to the sky
And then descends once more on to the earth
Receiving the strength of superior and inferior things.

"Le fils des étoiles" was produced at the Galerie Durand-Ruel on March 17, 1892, for a meeting of the Rosicrucians. The music proved to be far above their heads and was met by an icy silence. The program read as follows:

Erik Satie has composed three preludes for harps and flutes, admirably Oriental in character, which before each scene prepare the spectator tensely for what he is about to see. The same young composer is the author of several fanfares which, owing to the originality and the austerity of their style, have been adopted for the Order's ceremonies and which may not, unless the High Priest allows it, be played anywhere but at the Order's meetings.

Satie's three short preludes, delicate and pure, could not be understood by the critics of the time. As for the Rosicrucian "Sonneries," printed in red with a lovely illustration by Puvis de Chavannes, it is difficult to tell how often they were played at the meetings. Erik Satie was soon bored by so strict and serious an order. The Sâr believed firmly in the idealistic, and mystical art and jokes were not tolerated at the meetings over which he presided. Satie indicated his growing impatience by an amusing letter addressed to the editor of the paper "Gil Blas":

Paris, this fourteenth day of the month of August in the year '92
Master Editor,
Truly it doth amaze me that I, a poor wretch, having no thoughts but for my Art alone, should continually be proclaimed and hailed as Initiator in music of the disciples of Master Joséphin Péladan. This grieves and offends me sorely inasmuch as were I to be the pupil of whomsoever, methinks that whomsoever would be none other than myself; the more so since I hold to the belief that Master Péladan, for all the fullness of his learning, could never make disciples either in music, painting or in aught besides. Wherefore I declare the aforesaid Master Péladan, whom I hold truly in full respect and fitting deference, has never in any

wise exercised authority over the independence of my Aesthetic, and stands to me in the relation, not of Teacher but of Colleague, thus differing in no wise from my old friends Masters J.-P. Contamine de Latour and Albert Tinchant.

Before Holy Mary, Mother of Our Lord Jesus, Third Person of the Divine Trinity, I have spoken and declared, without hatred or evil intent, the View I take of such an intention; and I swear before the Fathers of the Holy Church that in all this I have not sought to do injury to, nor do I cherish any grievance against my friend Master Péladan.

Be so good, Master Editor, as to accept the humble salutations of a poor wretch, having no thoughts but for his Art alone, and grieved to have to deal with a question that causes him so much pain.[1]
Erik Satie

His collaboration with Tinchant may never have gone beyond the planning stage. A notice in the newspapers announced the presentation of an opera in three acts, libretto by Albert Tinchant, music by Erik Satie, to be presented at the Grand Théâtre in Bordeaux, entitled "Le Bâtard de Tristan"! Together with Contamine de Latour, Satie created "Uspud," a Christian ballet in three acts, dedicated to "The Supreme, Luminous, and Permanent Indivisibility of the Holy Trinity." A single character, Uspud, and a host of "spiritualities" comprise the cast. Uspud, in Persian costume, appears on a deserted beach. In the center is a statue; in the distance, the sea. In the second act, Uspud is converted, in his home, after having been attacked by demons with the heads of such animals as dogs, jackals, tortoises, goats, fish, lynx, tiger-wolves, oxen, sea-woodcocks,

[1] This translation of the letter appears in "Erik Satie," by Rollo H. Myers, on p. 131.

unicorns, sheep, antelopes, ants, spiders, gnus, snakes, blue "agouti-boucs," baboons, "cuculu," albatross, "pacre," ostriches, moles, secretary birds, old bulls, red caterpillars, "bouti," "pogos," boars, crocodiles buffaloes, etc. The third act is an apotheosis. Uspud, torn to pieces by the demons, is lifted up to Christ by the care of "the Christian Church." The authors sent their masterpiece to Bertrand, Director of the Opéra, who did not deign to acknowledge receipt of the precious manuscript in its little black folder. The composer, infuriated, brandished the regulations and sent Bertrand his seconds, challenging him to a duel. Deeply disturbed, Bertrand called to convince him politely not to go ahead with it. In 1895, the two accomplices published a little pamphlet containing the text and a few musical excerpts of "Uspud." A note on the cover indicated that "Uspud" had been "présente à" (presented *to* or *at*) the Théâtre National de l'Opéra on December 20, 1892! The same pamphlet announced the presentation in the near future of "Ontrotance," a ballet in one act, followed, "God willing," by three more: "Corcleru," "Irnebizolle," and "Tumisrudebude."

The association between Master Salis and his pianist did not last long. Erik left the "Chat-Noir" in a huff and was engaged as pianist by the "Auberge du Clou" on the Avenue Trudaine. Here it was that one night in 1891 appeared a young musician who had just received the Prix de Rome, Claude Achille Debussy. "The minute I saw him I was drawn to him irresistibly, and I wished to live near him for ever. For thirty years I was fortunate enough to see my dream come true." This friendship which brought the two together stemmed from their common aspirations. It is not known whether Debussy at that time knew the early compositions of his strange colleague.

This started the old dispute about Satie's influence on the great Claude Debussy! A rather pointless dispute: it might be of more value simply to quote the two musicians. Debussy repeated to Jean Cocteau a sentence of Satie's which "determined the esthetic of Pelléas":

The orchestra should not posture when an actor appears on the stage. Look: do the trees on the stage posture? It should be possible to create in the same way a musical setting, a musical climate in which the characters move and speak. No couplets, no leitmotiv—but a certain atmosphere like a painting by Puvis de Chavannes.

This is precisely the esthetic of "Le fils des étoiles." In a lecture on Debussy, Satie clearly described the first conversations between the two innovators:

Debussy's esthetic is linked to symbolism in many of his works; yet it is Impressionist in his œuvre as a whole. Forgive me, I beg you; was I not in part the cause of this? It is often said that I was.

Allow me to explain this:

When I first met him, at the beginning of our friendship, he was full of Moussorgsky and was searching very conscientiously for a path which however proved difficult to find. On this point I had a great advantage over him: 'prizes', whether of Rome or of any other place, did not weigh on me and slow me down, for I bear no such award on my shoulders. Indeed, I am a man of the same kind as Adam—the Adam of Paradise. He never won a prize—a lazy man, no doubt.

I was writing music for the "fils des étoiles" at that time, on a text by Joséphin Péladan, and I explained to Debussy the necessity for a Frenchman to disengage himself from the Wagnerian adventure, which does not correspond to our natural aspirations. And I pointed out to him that I was by no means anti-Wagnerian, but that it was necessary for us to have a music of our own—with no sauerkraut, if possible.

Why not make use of the descriptive approach that Claude Monet, Cézanne, Toulouse-Lautrec, and others are showing us? Why not transpose this approach into music? Nothing simpler. Are these not expressions?

Here was the basis of an excellent starting-point which could lead to certain and perhaps even profitable achievements. . . . Who could show him examples? Reveal new discoveries to him? Point out the ground to be explored? Supply him the results of past experiments? Who?

I do not wish to answer; all this does not interest me any longer.

As regards theoretical influence, the influence of harmony, of resolutions, it can be observed, recognized, discussed or completely denied, but fifty years from now no-one will speak of it any more. This book was not written to sing the praise of Erik Satie the prophet: it is precisely this quality which has been used to mask the real musical value of his compositions.

At the "Auberge du Clou" Satie met with painters and enjoyed this very much. In their company his sense of humor, his musical aesthetic and his Bohemian spirit flourished. He learned more about music from painters, he claimed, than from musicians. A romantic affair which he had with a young girl artist brought him closer still to the world of painters.

In June, 1892, Satie publicly flaunted his eccentricity and presented himself as a candidate for membership in the Académie des Beaux-Arts. Ernest Guiraud, Debussy's master, had died, and Satie in all seriousness asked that his name be included on the list of candidates for the vacant seat. It is said that Gustave Moreau alone showed any friendliness when the twenty-six-year-old musician would call. The music department rejected his candidacy. With admirable gravity he sent a list of his compositions to accompany his application: each one of his "Gymnopédies" was described as an orchestral suite.

That same year saw the last traces of Satie's collaboration with the Rosicrucians, the composition of a "Hymne au Drapeau" for Péladan's "Prince de Byzance." Satie's great love for religious forms and his ever growing sense of humor led him to build his own Church. To anger the Rosicrucians, he founded the Metropolitan Church of Art of Jesus the Conductor ("L'Eglise Métropolitaine d'Art de Jésus Conducteur"). The aim of the new church was to fight against those "who have neither convictions nor beliefs, not a thought in their souls nor a principle in their hearts." Erik Satie, "Parcier" and "Maître de Chapelle" from the height of his "Abbatiale" in the Rue Cortot, published violent diatribes against the culprits of "the esthetic and moral decadence of our times," or handed down major excommunications to his worst enemies, Lugné-Poé, Alfred Vallette, Alexandre Natanson, and especially

Henry Gauthier-Villars, alias Willy, "l'Ouvreuse du Cirque d'Eté." At the house of
Lamoureux, one day, the two men came to
blows, using fists and walking sticks. Thanks
to a small inheritance—which disappeared
ever so fast—Satie had his pamphlets printed
and for a brief period of time published a
paper, "Le Cartulaire de l'Eglise," in which
he gave free rein to his fantasy and his re-
sentments.

His knowlege of Gothic art helped him
organize his church and determine costumes
and hierarchy in great detail. In each
category, the figures for active partici-
pants were fixed rather liberally: the "Péné-
ants noirs convers" could number up to
1,600,000,000! In the meantime, the "Parcier," left penniless, had to live in a closet
that his landlord Bibet kindly let him use.

These religious occupations, however,
did not keep him away from music, and he
composed a number of delightful piano
pieces: "Préludes pour le Nazaréen," "Prélude d'Eginhardt," and the beautiful
"Prélude de la Porte Héroïque du Ciel"
for Jules Bois' "Drame ésotérique." During
this period, he became part of a group which
had formed around "Le Cœur," a review "of
esotericism, literature, science, and art,"
edited by Bois and decorated with naive and
pious pictures by Antoine de la Rochefou-
cault. Subjected to this kind of influence,
Satie's inspiration became very definitely
religious. Thus, after the "Danses gothiques," "Novena for the greater peace and
stronger serenity of my soul," he composed
his "Messe des pauvres" of which "Le

Cœur" published the "Prières des orgues"
introduced by a vibrant article by Conrad
Satie. Full of brotherly praise, this article
tells us that "of a transcendental idealism,
Satie professes only contempt for that real-
ism which obfuscates the minds of his con-
temporaries." And further, that "thus, Erik
Satie must hope for nothing but mockery and
indifference from the masses." Debussy had
shown his compositions to Chausson, "who
almost fainted." Erik was happy because the
kind Claude had given him the false hope
that his works would be played as early as
1893 at the Société Nationale. Several years
would have to pass before this fairly "progressive" group played Satie's "Gymnopédies," in Debussy's orchestrated version.

In 1894 and again in 1896 he requested
a seat in the Institute, when first Gounod's
and then Ambroise Thomas's seats became
vacant. But in vain, for he was ignored.
Justly indignant, he wrote a letter to Saint-
Saëns, which was published in the "Mene-
strel":

Paris, the 17th day of May of the year 1894. Erik
Satie, 'maître de chapelle de l'Eglise Métropolitaine d'Art de Jésus Conducteur' to M. Camille
Saint-Saens.
To express my indignation and to contribute to
his betterment.
Sir:
I have submitted my candidacy to your judgment
for the succession to M. Charles Gounod in your
Company. In so doing, I did not behave in a
wildly presumptuous way but I simply obeyed
the dictates of my conscience. A feeling of justice or, in its absence, simple politeness made me
believe that my candidacy, approved by God,
would be accepted by you. My distress was great
when I saw that you had forgotten solidarity in

Art in favor of vulgar preferences. Let those of my colleagues whom you have similarly insulted humble themselves: as for me, I will not give up my right to have at least my existence recognized. You can accuse me of one thing only: of not knowing myself as well as I know you. Even though I am far from you, you must not ignore me but on the contrary you must come nearer to me. In judging me from a distance and in making your decision you have acted as a criminal and have incurred damnation. Your aberration can only be due to your refusal to accept the ideas of the Century and to your ignorance of God, which is the direct cause of Esthetic decline.

I forgive you in Jesus Christ and embrace you in the grace of God.
Erik Satie
6, Rue Cortot

Twenty years later he told in the "Mémoires d'un Amnésique" how these three failures had caused him "much sorrow." "Messieurs Paladilhe, Dubois, and Lenepveu were preferred, for no reason whatsoever." It might have been a consolation for Satie to know that there is today no glory attached to the names of these three "immortals."

In 1898, Satie felt the need for a change of environment and moved to the other end of Paris, pitching his tent in the wasteland of the Parisian suburbs.

This part of the suburbs at that time still had a somewhat provincial charm. No middle-class villas, with their neat little gardens, but poor and dirty old houses, a crowd of filthy urchins to win Satie's heart: "One feels here the mysterious presence of Our Lady of Lowliness." At night, walking home from Montmartre, a hammer in his pocket, he would wander dreamily along the smelly

Arcueil
I withdraw.
Erik Satie

tanneries of Gentilly. "Everything around
them is so sad and tearful that it moves me
and pleases me, like a pale and beautiful
wolf, a kind wolf."

He found a large room in an imposing
building, very much like a barrack, on the
Rue Cauchy. Right under Satie's window in
this pot-bellied house, known as "The Four
Chimneys," was a wine-shop, where people
would dance on Saturdays and Sundays to
the sounds of an accordion. Satie rented the
room in October 1898 but did not move in
till later. At first he only spent a few nights
there, almost reluctantly. He was bothered
by mosquitoes "doubtless sent there by
Freemasons." Then, he moved his treasures
in; he used a wheelbarrow to carry "the
boards, the mattress, the chest, and the
bench," all the furniture he owned. From
the window of his "Home" he could see "a
cottage belonging to a lord of the region who
practices the trade of master mason." Behind it rose the tall trees of the Parc de
l'Ecole d'Arcueil. Music was not yet taught
at this school; the young boys followed the
strict teachings of the Dominicans.

Neighbors whispered when they met
this bearded, handsome young man, dressed
in gray velvet from head to toe, and took
him for a painter. But he would pass by,
speaking to no one. Indeed, he was seldom
in Arcueil and would only return—if at all
—in the early hours of the morning, to go to
sleep. Once a week, his clay pipe wrapped in
a newspaper, he went to the Rue Cardinet,
where Claude Debussy lived. Here a piano
was at his disposal. His days were spent in

Montmartre with his new friend Depaquit.
They worked out plans for collaboration but
never went through with them completely.
In the spring of 1899, Satie composed his
delightful "Jack-in-the-box" to accompany
a pantomime by Depaquit at the Comédie
Parisienne. He expected "one of those
coats that look like a frock coat." And he
added: "This pantaloonery consoles me a
little and will be my way of making faces at
the evil men who live in this world."

The first years of the nineteenth century
were for Satie a period of great poverty and
discouragement. To earn a little money he
occasionally accompanied his friend Vincent
Hyspa who would sing for "high society."
But this he considered as work "of a profound baseness." "Your suit, your fine old
shirts," he wrote his brother, "have made
it possible for me to indulge in this little sport." Unfortunately "Jack-in-the-box"
never left his room! Perhaps because of re-
sentment he never spoke of this delightful
composition or, when asked, said that he
had lost it. At times, in his letters to Conrad
Satie, his usual sense of fun would give way
to weariness:

I am bored to tears and to death; whatever I
timidly undertake fails with a boldness hitherto
unknown.
What else can I do but turn toward God and
point my finger at Him. I've come to believe that
the Old Man is even more stupid than he is
powerful.
What is new with you? Tell me about yourself, my little friend; your future is very different from mine, luckily for you. You shall have
a horse and a big carriage, open in the summer,

closed in the winter. And you shall go to and fro,
just like the fortunate people.

I clasp you to my poor breast.

Debussy's presence alone could console
him. "If I did not have Debussy, . . . I do
not know how I would manage to express
my poor thoughts, assuming that I still express them at all." He was disgusted by the
people around him, whose minds all worked
like the minds of businessmen. "I do not see
a single gentleman around me."

On top of discouragement came artistic
insecurity. Debussy, close by, had completed his "Pelléas." In a letter to his brother,
Erik commented: "You ask me about 'Pelléas et Mélisande'; I can only say this: it is
very elegant, absolutely perfect." Jean Cocteau quoted from a letter also written at
about this time: "Nothing more can be done
with that idea; I must search for something
else, or I am lost."

In the meantime, and because he had to
eat, he composed pieces which he described
as "de rudes saloperies," although deep in
his heart he probably loved them. For
Madame Paulette Darty he wrote waltzes,
charming and sentimental: "Je te veux,"
"Tendrement," and "La Diva de l'Empire,"
a fluid and delicate "intermezzo américain." For himself, or perhaps for Debussy,
he composed "Trois morceaux en forme de
poire," which anticipated Satie's imminent
divorce from Impressionism. The story
behind these beautiful piano pieces is well
known. Debussy said one day to Satie that
he should develop his sense of form; this

piece of advice was met by an enigmatic little smile. A few weeks later, Satie showed up with his three pieces "in the form of a pear."

Gradually he got used to Arcueil and began to try out the restaurants of the area. He chatted with the local folk but remained very reserved. At last, he found a cheap eating place where he was very well treated. Perhaps too well; he stopped going there because "old mother Geng" was overwhelmingly nice to him, which he found irritating. He installed himself in a café across the street from the church, and there he remained a faithful customer.

He had arranged his mysterious room with great care. He did his own cleaning and waxed the floor himself. He soon tired of these chores; later he transferred this meticulous care to his clothes. His tattered curtains gave rise to unfriendly curiosity among his neighbours. He stopped opening his window when he noticed that curious neighbors were using binoculars to explore his room. In the evenings, pitcher in hand, he would go to draw water from the fountain in the Place des Ecoles. No other human being ever set foot in his room.

1905 found him collaborating with Maurice de Féraudy. He wrote parts of a musical comedy entitled "Pousse l'Amour."[2] During one rehearsal he lost his temper and stormed out, banging the door behind him.

The same year he made the humble and brave resolution to resume his musical

[2] Performed in Monte Carlo in 1913, under the title "Coco chéri!"

education.[3] He decided to enter the Schola
Cantorum, the austere and rigid school that
Debussy disliked. Although together they
had made fun of the "Prix de Rome," which
they had humorously characterized "brevet
d'origine d'instruction et d'authenticité de
premier choix," their views differed when
it came to public instruction, which according to Satie "leads to the most de-
testable vulgarity."

Debussy warned him to be careful, for
he was playing a dangerous game; at his age
it was too late to shed an old skin for a new
one. To this, Satie replied: "At worst, I
will fail, and that will mean that I had
nothing in me."[4]

He was very well received by Vincent
d'Indy at the Schola, where he entered
Serieyx's and Albert Roussel's classes. The
latter tried to dissuade Satie from resuming
his studies:

Satie was a professional musician. Those of his
works that had already been printed clearly
showed me that he had nothing to learn. I could
not see what advantages he could derive from
theoretical and academic studies. Nevertheless,
he insisted. He became a very docile and assiduous student. He would punctually bring me the
work I had assigned, carefully written out and
adorned with notes in red ink. He was pro-
foundly musical.

At the end of three years he left the
Schola, having obtained his Diploma in
counterpoint. He had now "fulfilled the con-

[3] The only other such instance known to us is that of
Glinka, who retired to Germany to study counterpoint
after the failure of "Russlan and Ludmilla."
[4] Quoted by Jean Cocteau.

ditions required for devoting oneself exclusively to composition." At the time he
was 42 years old.

Satie had kept the exercises he had composed for his classes at the Schola. After
his death, his brother Conrad gave them to
Darius Milhaud. They testify to the conscien-
tious and methodical efforts of the student
Satie, which were to "allow his inspiration
to lean on the wonderful technique which
brought such a transformation to contem-
rary musical thought."

At Arcueil by that time he had a number
of good friends who persuaded him to join
the local Radical-Socialist Committee. Satie
never missed a meeting. Ordinarily he
would sit in a corner, smoking quietly and
watching the various speakers. But he was
very excited by the idea of creating a *laic
patronage,* a nonreligious charitable organization, which brought him into close contact with children, whom he adored. Satie
would take them out on excursions. Some
still remember a visit to the fort of Bicêtre,
where Satie asked all manner of questions
of the soldiers. He organized concerts and
"fêtes" (admission fees: 0.50 fr. and 1 fr.).
For his participation in all these activities
he received well-deserved recognition at a
ceremony held on the 4th of July 1909: Monsieur de Selves, Prefect of the Seine, decorated him with the "Palmes Académiques"
for civic services. The local newspaper,
"L'Avenir d'Arcueil-Cachan," described the
informal reception which followed:

A small reception, as intimate as it was charming,
was held on the 8th of last month at the home of

M. Douau in the Rue Emile-Raspail. About
fifty people were gathered to honor M. Satie, who
had just received a decoration.

M. Cousin, representing the Municipality,
congratulated the newly elevated M. Satie and
recalled the services he had rendered to the interesting activities of the *laic patronage*. M.
Poensin, Vice-Chairman of the *patronage*, presented him with the silver palms, decorated
with rubies, which were offered by a group of
friends. Then M. Cormeray made the last of a
series of speeches.

M. Bladier sat down at the piano, played a
few notes, and gave the signal for the musical
part of the reception to begin; M. and Mme.
Bravard brought to us with professional vir-
tuosity two charming melodies composed by
Erik Satie, "Je te veux" and "Tendrement." Need-
less to say, these met with enthusiastic applause.

Our friend Piaulet, vivacious as ever, had
the audience laughing to the point of tears with
his monologues, as amusing as they were brilliantly executed.

Indeed, soon all were following his example,
and each put on his little show and sang his little
song. Dancing went on till three in the morning.

The newspaper informed its readers that
M. Satie's solfeggio classes were held every
Sunday at 10 a.m. Satie was very active; he
organized a concert that was long remem-
bered by his awed fellow-citizens. He se-
cured the collaboration of Vincent Hyspa
and Madame Paulette Darty, who interpreted various of his works. The "musical
proficiency" of Satie, the Honorary Chairman of the Committee of Art Students and
Director of the Internal Services of the *laic
patronage* was said to be "equaled only by
his devotion to the works of the *patronage*."
The concert was a tremendous success. "Is
it necessary to tell you that the hall was
literally exploding with applause? Satie, at

the piano, smiled into his beard. It was for all a delightful, artistic evening."

Soon Satie founded a regional group comprising Normandy, Maine, Anjou, and Poitou. (Satie's love for this kind of organization was in strange contrast to his desire for solitude.) Then he became a contributor to the local newspaper, for which he wrote regularly the "Quinzaine des Sociétés." Here one could find little notices which needed not be signed to be immediately identifiable as Satie's:

BEING BITTEN BY A MONKEY
is less fun than a visit to 60 Rue Emile-Raspail —chez l'Ami Jacob—the dancing school "La Marguerite."

NO MORE BALD HEADS
if everyone joined the new Savings Society "L'Aqueduc." You can use your earnings to buy a hair lotion.

YOU ARE BEING DECEIVED
if you do not know that M. Ollinger-Jacob, the famous Director of the world's greatest movie theater, expects you every Saturday at 8.30, in his superb salons. Monsieur Ollinger-Jacob has received a number of fictitious orders and decorations; he has been commissioned by the Imperial Court of the Sahara, by his Greatness the Doge of Manchester and by his Grandness the Sultan of Livarot. Immense pleasure guaranteed; you always have fun.

But the new Director of the *patronage* soon resigned, advancing the first pretext he could think of: "a stranger on the managing board took the liberty of distorting, through contemptible gossip, the facts under discussion." But he was sad to leave his children. They followed him around in the streets; whenever he could afford to, he gave them a few pennies. The following year he found a way to take children out on excursions, delightedly listening to them and telling them stories. A letter to the Mayor shows his great kindness:

Arcueil-Cachan, August 4, 1910
Dear Sir,
The Municipality of Arcueil-Cachan is organizing —as it has in past years—an excursion for the children of the summer course. The funds at the Municipality's disposal make it necessary to limit the number of children who will take part in this pleasant outing.

In order to remedy at least in part these regrettable circumstances, I have been able to put together, with the help of some friends, a sum of money that will make it possible for a few more children—to be exact, for twelve children, six boys and six girls—to enjoy a diversion which is so seldom offered them.

I therefore wish to ask you to authorize me to take with me the twelve children whom I have chosen.

I attach a list of these children, so that the Directors of the Schools will not include them on their own lists. With the authorization of the children's parents, I will take full responsibility for the care and the conduct of the children who will be entrusted to me.

This excursion was the last educational activity in which this apostle took part before his involvement with the "Nouveaux Jeunes" and with the "Groupe des Six." At this time of his tormented life, he was in dire straits; poverty had come, he said, "like a sad little girl, with big green eyes."

Recognition   By the end of 1910, Maurice Ravel and a few of Satie's friends, in whose hands lay the destiny of the recently formed *Société Musicale Indépendante* (S.M.I.), decided to present to the public the early piano works of the little-known musician. Satie explained the reasons for this in a letter he wrote to his brother:

In 1905 I began to study with d'Indy. I was tired of being reproached for an ignorance that I believed myself in truth to be guilty of, since competent people had pointed to it in my works.

At the end of three years' hard work, I received from the Schola Cantorum a diploma in counterpoint, signed by my excellent teacher, who is certainly the best and the most learned man in the world. So there I was, in 1908, holding a degree conferring on me the right to call myself contrapuntist. Very proud of my newly acquired knowledge, I began to compose. My first composition of this kind was a Chorale and Fugue for four hands. I've often been insulted in the course of my sad existence, but never before had I been so despised. Why on earth had I gone to d'Indy? The things I had written before were so full of charm. And now? What nonsense! What dullness!

Thereupon, "the young ones" organized an anti-d'Indy movement and decided to play the "Sarabandes," "Le fils des étoiles," etc., the same works that were once considered the fruits of my great ignorance - quite wrongly, according to the same "young ones."

And that, my dear fellow, is the way life goes.

It's all very confusing.

Maurice Ravel ("He assures me every time I see him that he owes me a great deal. Delighted, I'm sure.") insisted on playing Satie's compositions personally at a concert given by the *Société Musicale Indépendante* on January 16, 1911. The second "Sarabande," a prelude from "Le fils des étoiles," and the third "Gymnopédie" were performed and were given a friendly reception.

The biographical notice in the program paid tribute to the "explorer":

Erik Satie occupies a truly exceptional place in

the history of contemporary art. On the fringe of
his age and in isolation he wrote, years ago, a few
brief pages that bear the stamp of an inspired
pioneer. His works, regrettably few in number,
astonish by the way in which they anticipated
the modern idiom and by the near-prophetic
character of certain harmonic inventions . . . .
. . . M. Claude Debussy paid a brilliant tribute to the "explorer" when he orchestrated two
of his "Gymnopédies," which have since been
performed at the Société Nationale. Today, M.
Maurice Ravel will play the second "Sarabande,"
which bears the astonishing date of 1887, and will
thus indicate what high esteem the most "progressive" composers have for the creator who
spoke, a quarter of a century ago, the bold musical "jargon" of tomorrow.

Debussy, who was on bad terms with
Maurice Ravel and was upset because he had
been left out of his old friend's triumph,
sulked. "One who isn't very happy is good
old Claude. He has no one to blame for it
but himself; had he done earlier what Ravel
has done, his position would now be different." The "progressive" press, repre-
sentative of the young school, pounced on
Satie; D. Calvocoressi and Jules Ecorcheville
wrote excellent articles, and Erik Satie was
thrilled and moved by his small triumph.
Several months later, Debussy conducted
Satie's "Gymnopédies" at the "Cercle Musical" and was surprised by their success.
"Why will he not leave me a little place in
his shade? I do not aspire to the sun." This
new hostility could not but grow with the
passing of time and the deepening of their
esthetic rivalry.

Satie was happy, but extremely poor.
At a concert of the S.M.I. in June 1912, the
"Prélude de la porte héroïque du ciel,"

orchestrated by Roland-Manuel (the young-
est of his admirers), was performed; Satie
did not attend because he was so "shabbily
dressed." This delicate composition created
a sensation. In the audience were a few
"Satieists"—"they are no more comical
than the Wagnerians." Satie was presented
as a candidate for the title of "Prince of
Musicians," his candidacy backed by the
young coterie. Satie commented: "He won't
be very rich, this Prince of Musicians, poor
fellow."

Success had given him new courage,
and he began working once more. In 1911
he composed two fugues and two chorales
for orchestra, "En Habit de Cheval" ("In
riding gear"), the enigmatic title of which
doubtless evokes the freedom with which he
overrides rules. Later he explained that the
clothes alluded to were those not of the rider
but of the horse, "for instance: . . . two shafts
attached to a four-wheel carriage." He may
have been thinking of the rules which "do-
mesticate" musicians. He searched for a
libretto, but his imagination demanded a
great deal from his collaborators. Unsuccessful in this search, he decided to create a
libretto himself. His works were now sought
after by publishers: Rouart-Lerolle published his earlier compositions, "Sarabandes," "Gymnopédies," "Porte héroïque
du ciel," "Le fils des étoiles." Dements asked
him for some piano pieces: Satie responded
·with "Trois préludes flasques (pour un
chien)" ["Three flabby preludes (for a dog)"],
but this enlightened publisher did not like
them. Delighted to have his works pub-

lished—and to earn fifty francs—Satie put these back in his files and brought more, which appeared as the "Véritables préludes flasques" ("'Real' flabby preludes"). This was the first of a series of collections of piano pieces, imaginative and charming, intended to be comical and to ridicule the exaggerately sweet lyricism of "good old Claude's" preludes and the outmoded symbolism of the titles he gave them. Thus appeared a set of small gems, such as "Croquis et agaceries d'un gros bonhomme en bois," "Embryons desséchés," "Enfantillages pittoresques" —in which he proved his talent as a children's musician—and "Sports et divertissements." He composed these beautiful pieces at a little table in a café in Arcueil. He would arrive at about eleven in the morning, drink a beer, smoke his cigars, have lunch, chat with the other clients and suddenly bring from his pocket one of his little notebooks. Oblivious to all, he would slowly cover the score with well-formed notes. Friends would greet him, but he would not answer; yet the next day he would seriously accuse them of bad manners. Readers of the journal of the S.M.I. began to look out for installments of "Les Mémoires d'un Amnésique" ("Memoirs of an Amnesiac") in which he gave free rein to his comical verve. Perhaps the most memorable of these were the famous notes on "A Musician's Day," often reproduced in anthologies. Ricardo Viñes, the great pianist, would include on the program of each of his performances some of Satie's little pieces; these would invariably elicit an encore. People laughed and listened to them inattentively, and their beauty passed almost unnoticed. But isn't that precisely what the composer wanted?

The war broke out. Claude Debussy was bewildered, crushed, unable to compose anything. Satie, with the egoism of the free artist, paid no serious attention to what went on at the front. He allied himself with the socialist party and pretended to participate actively. He joined the fierce groups of citizen-soldiers who scoured the streets of the suburbs. To him this was an opportunity for delightful nightly strolls in the course of which he mocked the cowards who went around armed to the teeth . . . . Later, during the air raids on Paris, he would regularly go and knock at a friend's door and whisper: "I have come to die with you." He would laugh and joke, and his pince-nez would fall off. Perhaps he wasn't completely unconcerned. "I am really happy to come here," he would say, "at home, I would have to spend the night under the mattress."

He became more and more successful as a musician; an important place was by now reserved to his works at performances. At times, whole concerts would be devoted to him. At one of these, Roland Manuel gave a refined, if affected, talk. Satie met Cocteau and composed "Cinq grimaces" for his adaptation of "Songe d'une nuit d'été," which was never performed.

Satie's collaboration with Cocteau for the ballet "Parade" dates back to the spring of 1915. Cocteau was a close friend of Serge Diaghilev's. Fascinated by the "Morceaux en

Parade

On attendait le rouleau; nous n'avons que le ballet.
L'Oeuvre, May 20, 1917

forme de poire," Cocteau showed Erik Satie a project for a ballet which he had already presented, in a different version and under the title "David," to Igor Stravinsky. "Gradually, a composition evolved in which Satie seems to have discovered an unknown dimension enabling one to hear at the same time both the 'parade' and the show going on inside." His collaborator left for Rome with Pablo Picasso, who had seriously compromised his position with the artists of Montparnasse by agreeing to paint the scenery and the costumes for "Parade."

In Rome, Diaghilev and his troupe were waiting for them. Here Picasso conceived shapes and colors that were destined to revolutionize the esthetic of theatrical sets, while at the same time Massine worked on a choreography which was to transform the spirit of Russian ballet. Far from them, Satie was hard at work on the simplest score possible, reacting, perhaps unknowingly, against the Debussyism and fauvism of which "Le Sacre du Printemps" had marked the peak.

After a series of stormy rehearsals, in which Satie was not always enthralled by his main collaborator's "inventions," "Parade" was presented at the Châtelet, on May 18, 1917, at a gala performance for a war charity. "No miracle was ever accomplished without the help of faith," was M. Laloy's comment on this première. The public in this third year of the war was hardly prepared to do justice to the meaning of a composition that revolutionized the conception of ballet. It was a scandal: all

Paris was at the Châtelet and the audience was in an uproar. Satie was delighted; they were fighting over him! Up to then, except for his supposedly humorous compositions, his works had been met politely, or even coldly. He had celebrated his fifty-first birthday the day before! To some extent, it is true, the authors had asked for a scandal; the program was full of aggressive pronouncements, such as Appollinaire's statement on the "New Spirit," and strange rumors had spread prior to the performance. The press reacted beautifully, stigmatizing Satie, Cocteau, and Picasso as *boches*. Gaston Carraud claimed that "Parade" was "a vivid illustration on the stage and in the audience of the war spirit characteristic of certain Parisian social spheres." And M. Poueigh, whose only claim to fame has been this article—solemnly declared, " . . . and, in any case, the times in which we are living are badly chosen for such escapades." Not to mention M. Pierre Lalo, who was once more mistaken.

A review by one of these pompous critics sent the composer into such a rage that he began mailing him insulting postcards. Brought to court, the author was condemned to 8 days in prison for "public insults and slander." There was a stormy hearing, at which Jean Cocteau defended his friend not only with his voice but also with his fists.

This sudden fame, this scandalous glory led to a final break with Claude Debussy. "Our horizons moved from one hour to the next," wrote Satie, after Debussy's death.

M. Laloy, who was a friend of the latter and an enemy of the first, has clearly explained this separation:

Debussy was unhappy, crushed by events, slowly consumed by an illness of which nothing could stop the slow poison, deeply absorbed in bitter thoughts and more than ever incapable of making an effort to be congenial and to offer courteous praise. By the time concerts were organized for Satie and devoted exclusively to Satie's works, he was already restricted to his room and unable to attend. Tales of Satie's success left him suspicious, fearing a hoax. Satie guessed this from Debussy's words and was so embittered that he wrote Debussy an almost insulting letter. Debussy received it in the bed to which he had been confined for several weeks and where he was to die soon after. His unsteady hands crumpled the piece of paper on his lap, inadvertently ripping it. "I'm sorry!", he murmured, like a child about to be scolded, with tears in his eyes. I could never forgive Satie for having caused a pain of which he could not possibly have foreseen the cruelty. Only after his death, seven years later, did I forgive him, having learned from his friends how bitterly he too must have suffered at a time when others were praising him while the praise that most mattered to him in the world was denied him. Thus, throught the fault of both, ended miserably their friendship.

A few weeks before his death, Satie, who had been impatient with Roger Desormière over some trifling matter, begged to be forgiven in very touching words, saying to him: "How Debussy must have suffered because of me while he was ill."

It was after the adventure with "Parade" that the younger musicians spontaneously drew closer to Satie. In June 1917, a concert program listed, along with Satie's name, those of George Auric, Louis Durey, and Arthur Honegger. This concert was given

at 6, Rue Huyghens, in the studio of a
friendly painter. It had been Blaise Cen-
drars' idea to assemble here, in Lejeune's
home, those artists who professed the "New
Spirit." Satie then decided to organize the
group and founded a society, "Les Nouveaux
Jeunes." The group gave a series of concerts
at the Vieux-Colombier, which was directed
by Madame Jane Bathori; and their oldest
member ("*my* youth is in my character")
gave brilliant and amusing talks. He introduced Germaine Tailleferre, "our Marie
Laurencin," Auric, Durey, Honegger. "We
have no Chairman, nor do we have a trea-
surer, or an archivist, or a manager. But then
we have no treasure. That makes it all very
easy for us." At the concerts organized by
the "Nouveaux Jeunes" a few compositions
by a prolific and forceful musician, a friend
of Honegger's, Darius Milhaud were performed. Soon Jean Cocteau joined the youth-
ful group, intrigued by this new generation
of musicians, "who no longer blink, who do
not wear masks, do not deny, do not hide,
do not fear to love nor to defend what they
love." "Le Coq et l'arlequin" ("Cock and
Harlequin"), a beautiful book in which
Satie's mischievous smile hides behind
each sentence, was dedicated to Georges
Auric.

But Satie was already turning his back
on the aphorisms of the "Coq": "There is
a hope that we may soon have an orchestra
with no caressing strings. A rich chorus of
wood, brass, and percussion instruments."
The verve of "Parade," "an 'orpheon' loaded
with dreams," no longer interested its au-

thor. "Socrate" was already taking shape in his mind.

Socrate and its disciples

I completely agree with our detractors. It is regrettable to see artists make use of publicity. Yet Beethoven was not unskillful with his publicity. It is thanks to this that he became well known, I think.
Erik Satie

In the spring of 1918, Debussy was dying a very painful death, far from his old friend who was calmly absorbing the scandal of "Parade" and planning new compositions. Madame Bathori, who had convinced him two years earlier to write melodies ("Daphénéo," "La Statue de bronze," "Le Chapelier"), suggested to the Princess de Polignac that she commission the new and fashionable maestro to compose something for her. Thus it was that Satie wrote "Socrate" within the space of a few months. It is difficult to know whether the idea of writing a "symphonic drama" based on Plato's "Dialogues" came to his mind suddenly or whether it had been maturing for a long time. Once more, one must take into account his astonishing intuition. Perhaps Satie attended a Montjoie festival held in February 1918, at which his faithful friend Pierre Bertin read some excerpts from the *Banquet*, translated by Mario Meunier. This performance, the theme of which was "the soul of antiquity in modern society," was concluded with a brief concert in which Ricardo Viñes played a "Gymnopédie," a "Gnossienne," and a "Sarabande." Did Satie see a reflection of himself in Socrates?

One wonders also whether Satie would have written this serious and fervent work while "good old Claude" was still alive. In a sense, Debussy's death may have been a liberation for Satie. His "gentle and admiring" friendship may have weighed on the musician, who had little faith in himself and did not dare express himself seriously, fearing his friend's comments. The separation and Debussy's death allowed Satie, who at the time was no more than the author of "Parade," to write something into which he would put "the best of himself."

Never had Satie been so happy: he was now invited everywhere, respected, and esteemed. A little dazzled by the large sums —large in his eyes—that passed into his hands,[4] he now bought shirt-collars, umbrellas, handkerchiefs; he could at last buy presents for his friends. Madame Balguerie sang "Socrate" for the "tout-Paris" and the author, accompanying her, had his revenge for all the times when he had accompanied his old friend Hyspa for this same audience.

Darius Milhaud returned from Brazil, loaded with rhythms and melodies. By then the "Nouveaux Jeunes" had broken up, but the friendship between the two resumed. Among the musicians who surrounded Satie a newcomer had appeared: Francis Poulenc, whose "Rhapsodie Nègre" had met with a tremendous success at the Vieux-Colombier. They would all get together at the homes of Cocteau, Milhaud, or Pierre Bertin. Cocteau wrote for "Paris-Midi" to keep the readers up to date on "the flow of new values." The studio in the Rue Huyghens had become famous: Delgrange would hold concerts here at which all the "fashionable" would show

[5] "If the dead vanish fast, money, which is no more stupid than anything else, vanishes as fast as they do; and it's a pleasure to see it go, straight ahead, with never a glance behind and proud as a peacock for all that." (Letter to his brother.)

up. "People either freeze or die of heat, cramped together, sitting and standing, one against the other, just like at the Nord-Sud." Bertin sang the melodies with deep intelligence, Marcelle Meyer and Ricardo Viñes brought life to the pianos. Delgrange conducted "Parade" at Gaveau's, after Beethoven, Schubert, Fauré, and Debussy's "La mer." Satie was praised for the wrong reasons and was presented against his will as being opposed to Impressionism and even to his friend Stravinsky. He was not taken in, however, and he worked hard at his beautiful nocturnes.

"Socrate" was first performed publicly in January 1920 at the Société Nationale. Those who could not understand it boldly insulted the composer, and others simply took the whole thing to be a great joke. Satie immediately got back to work and composed "Trois petites pièces montées." After the performance of "Socrate," M. Henry Collet wrote an article for "Comœdia", entitled "The Five Russians, the Six French, and M. Erik Satie." Thus artificially lumped together under this lucky number, Germaine Tailleferre, Auric, Durey, Honegger, Milhaud, and Poulenc willy-nilly became a solid entity. This was extremely advantageous for those of the group who had little talent. Jean Cocteau, champion of the Six, founded "Le Coq," a review of "mutual admiration," which was printed on poster paper. "Le Coq," which was supposed to "reeducate" the spirit, was full of Satie's malicious attacks and outbursts; from time to time, however, he would be serious:

I never attack Debussy. It is the Debussysts who irritate me. There is no such thing as a School of Satie. Satieism could never exist. I would be opposed to it.

In art there must be no slavery. With each new composition, I have tried to baffle any followers I may have had, as regards both the form and the contents of my works. Only thus can an artist avoid becoming the leader of a "school"—that is to say, a pundit.

Let us thank Cocteau for the help he is giving us in escaping the habits of provincial and professorial boredom of the recent Impressionist compositions.

The margins are full of delightfully impertinent remarks: "To think that this kind of rubbish gets printed and that a man like Henry Bordeaux cannot find a publisher!" The Dada school was still alive. "Littérature," its official magazine, liquidated other values by establishing an average of the grades given to the celebrities of the time. Satie, who had obtained almost the same grades as Landru, was appreciated by Aragon and by Breton; he came in second among the musicians with an average of 2.72, while Debussy's negative grade put him on the same level as Anatole France and Marshal Foch. These slightly morbid games, popular in the period immediately following the war, amused Satie. But the musician would escape from his followers and from himself by drawing, with meticulous care, strange and cryptic little figures. In the company of young musicians he felt at ease, and his great love for music was nourished by the hopes he had for their future:

I had the pleasure of meeting myself last Monday at Darius Milhaud's, where I was lunching with Auric.

I was indeed very happy to find myself in the company of these two great artists, for whom I have a very deep affection.

Yes, dear friend, these two artists are my consolation for the future and even for the present.

I am extremely pleased to know that they are there, strong and bold.

I shall always go along with these two men, so full of firm courage.

The musique d'ameublement

Toute idée est une belle occasion de se taire. Elle est perdue.
Léon-Paul Fargue

On the 8th of March 1920, at the Galerie Barbazanges in the Faubourg Saint-Honoré, Pierre Bertin, the untiring organizer, introduced Satie's invention in the following words:

We are presenting today for the first time a creation of Messieurs Erik Satie and Darius Milhaud, directed by M. Delgrange, the "musique d'ameublement" ("furnishing music") which will be played during the intermissions. We urge you to take no notice of it and to behave during the intervals as if it did not exist. This music, specially composed for Max Jacob's play ("Ruffian, toujours; truand, jamais") claims to make a contribution to life in the same way as a private conversation, a painting in a gallery, or the chair on which you may or may not be seated. You will be trying it out. MM. Erik Satie and Darius Milhaud will be at your disposal for any information or commissions.

There had been the "musique à l'emporte-pièce," characterized by "plainness and clearly defined outlines"; objectivism was also a fashionable word; but Satie pushed to an extreme his reaction against the type of music to which one listens "with one's head in one's hands." A piano, three clarinets, and a trombone scattered in the corners of the hall ceaselessly repeated popular refrains. This idea, so full of possibilities, was looked upon as a joke. This was not true, however, and its esthetic importance was real. It was after all nothing but the extension, the exaggeration of principles which Satie had applied in "Le fils des étoiles": a motionless, decorative music. As we shall see later, this was the meaning he wished to give "Socrate." The "musique d'ameublement" soon found its real significance in film music, which one should not listen to, but which in spite of itself should contribute to the emotional content of the film (see the "Entr'acte" of "Relâche"). Not to mention the unexpected emergence of radio, where music becomes, for the wireless lover, an accompaniment to his meal, to a book, to conversation; he does not listen to it, but it is nonetheless necessary to him. It is difficult to know how serious Satie was about his invention. In a small notebook where he had copied the words of "Socrate," one can find these mysterious tables:

The banquet—'Musique d'ameublement' —For an assembly-hall.	Frame (dance) Tapestry (the Banquet, subject) Frame (dance, reprise)
Phèdre—'Musique d'ameublement' —For a lobby.	Colonnade (dance) Bas-relief (marble, subject) Colonnade (dance, reprise)
Phédon—'Musique d'ameublement' —For a shop window.	Casket (pig-down, dance) Cameo (Asian Agate—Phédon, subject) Casket (dance, reprise)

After the "Pièces montées," which enjoyed a genuine success in February 1920 at the Comédie des Champs-Elysées, Satie composed for Mademoiselle Caryathis "La belle excentrique," a serious fantasy "costumed by Poiret," reminiscent of a turn-of-the-century cancan. Then he took a rest. He was commissioned to do several works but never wrote them. He was asked, in particular, to write the music for the ballet "La naissance de Vénus," for which his friend Derain was going to paint the sets, and the score for "Paul et Virginie," based on a libretto by Jean Cocteau and Raymond Radiguet. He led all his friends to believe that the opera had been completed, but after his death nothing was found.

He published numerous articles in such magazines as "Action," "Feuilles libres," "Vanity Fair"; with wit and irony he fought many a battle in his slightly complicated style, and he was right more often than not. Nobody was spared: the "Périmés" (the "obsolete ones"), the critics, the "Six," Stravinsky himself. After making thousands of excuses, he finally agreed to go to Brussels and to Ghent, where he gave several talks. This trip to Belgium was the occasion for more than one fantastic eccentricity, for violent storms, and heroic sulks.

"Le Piège de Méduse, Comedy in one act by M. Erik Satie (with music by the same gentleman)" was written in 1913. It is a somewhat heavy farce, in which, however, Satie appears once more as a "forerunner," this time of the Dadaist and surrealist theaters. Baron Méduse, in order to test the sincerity of Astolfo, the suitor of his foster-daughter Frisette, sets a gross trap for him. Astolfo proves to be sincere; he wins Frisette. The other characters are Polycarpe, an arrogant servant who addresses his master

with great familiarity, and the monkey
Jonas, "stuffed by a master of the art,"
who between the scenes dances to delightful
music. Bertin produced "Le Piège de Méduse" at his "Théâtre Bouffe" in May 1921.
Satie was upset, because he thought he
recognized himself in Méduse . . . .

Early in 1923, Darius Milhaud introduced Satie to four young musicians who
greatly admired him: Cliquet-Pleyel, Roger
Désormière, Maxime-Jacob and Henry Sauguet. Satie received them very warmly and
introduced them to the public at the Collège de France and then at the Théâtre de
l'Atelier. So grateful were they to Satie that
they adopted the title of "L'Ecole d'Arcueil."
The elegance of the aging maestro was
veiled by melancholy and gentleness in the
talks he gave to introduce his young friends:

Myself, I have always had faith in youth . . . To
this day, I have had no cause to regret it . . . It is
true, I have not always been paid back punctually . . . No matter, I continue to have faith.

Our times are favorable to the young. Let
them beware nonetheless . . . Their youth will
be used to attack them.

One does not have to be very subtle to notice that people of a certain age always speak of
their experience . . . That's very kind of them . . .
But one ought to be sure that they do have some
experience . . . .

Man's memory is very short . . . How often
have we not heard, whenever the weather be-
haves in an unusual way: "There has never been
anything like this within living memory . . . "

I am quite willing to believe them; . . . but
let them not speak to me of their experience . . . of
their perspicacity . . . I know them—I even recognize them.

. . . And so, these young people will be reproached for their youth . . . I composed my

"Sarabandes" at the age of twenty-one, in 1887, and my "Gymnopédies" at twenty-two, in 1888.

These are the only works that my detractors admire - those over fifty, of course . . . To be logical, they should like the music I wrote as a mature man, as a 'compatriot'. But no . . .

In 1923, Satie composed five lovely melodies based on Léon-Paul Fargue's "Ludions", and set to music some dialogues for Gounod's "Le Médecin malgré lui." In Monte Carlo, Serge Diaghilev organized an opera season and asked the musicians of the French school to write recitatives for some of Gounod's and Chabrier's less known musical comedies. Satie made a quick trip to join the Russian troupe, broke unexpectedly with Auric and Poulenc, and returned to Paris.

He then drew closer to his friends in Montparnasse—Francis Picabia, Marcel Duchamp—and wrote for their journals: "391" and "Paris-Journal."

Mercure and Relâche

Cultivate in yourself that for which the public reproaches you; it is your true self.
Jean Cocteau

In 1924 Satie made his greatest effort, an effort which exhausted him. In spring, he composed "Mercure"; and in autumn, "Relâche."

"Mercure" had been commissioned by the Count de Beaumont, who at the "Cigale" Theater organized a series of performances of "advanced" ballets and plays, grouped under the title "Soirées de Paris." Massine, who was the choreographer for the "Soirées," had presented to Satie his concept of "plastic poses." Picasso painted splendid costumes as well as brilliantly fantastic sets and constructions. The première, on June 15, 1924, was clamorous; demonstrations against the musician and the painter created an aggressive atmosphere. The press was hard on Satie, but he had expected it. One of the most violent "critics" was precisely Satie's favorite, Georges Auric. But the score did not really become known till five years after the musician's death.

Francis Picabia showed his friend Satie his notes for an "instantanéiste" ballet of his creation. His audacity, which appeared as something novel to Satie, delighted him. He could not offer the project to Diaghilev, who would not have been interested, and therefore thought of Rolf de Maré's Swedish Ballet, which in 1923 ha produced the beautiful "Création d Monde" by Milhaud and Léger.

The more inventions people bring to him, the happier de Maré is; he certainly does not seek scandal for its own sake, but he does not fear it if that which may provoke it is worthwhile in his opinion. I think he even prefers it to the atmosphere created by a certain public which "understands" modern things in the same way in which devout people accept the miracles of Lourdes.

And Picabia added: "Art becomes a pleasure."

This phrase became the slogan of the last season of the Swedish ballet. A program-manifesto exalted life and provoked the audience. The following words appeared under Picabia's portrait: "I would rather hear them scream than clap." They screamed. The first performance was scheduled for November 27, but "Relâche," which can mean simply "no performance," lived up to its title; the curtain did not go up that night. Was this a new provocation? Three days later the curtain did rise, and the show went on. René Clair's film, which was certainly of great interest, stimulated the indignation of the Old School, but the ballet and the gloomy dances by Jean Borlin and his companions were not as unsuccessful as Picabia had hoped. The scenery for the second act bore inscriptions such as "Erik Satie is the greatest musician in the world" and "If you don't like it, the box office will sell you whistles for two cents." Only when the authors appeared on stage in a tiny 5-HP. automobile did the serious people become irritated. The press became violent in its attacks. Meanwhile, the musician was gradually succumbing to his illness.

And after all, long live life, right?
Picabia

His friends in Arcueil watched him gradually lose his strength and grow thinner. He could no longer climb into the Châtelet streetcar. They realized that he was ill one night, when he had invited them to dinner before taking them to see "Relâche." He hardly touched any food and drank only mineral water . . . After that, he disappeared; and six months later they read of his death in the newspapers.

He would spend his days with Braque, with Derain, or with Milhaud. At Milhaud's home, he would sit by the fireplace, the collar of his overcoat turned up, his hat on his head, and would not move. Pleurisy was sapping all his strength; his friends persuaded him with difficulty not to go back to Arcueil. With Jean Wiener's help he took a room at the Grand-Hôtel, but boredom increased his pain:

He would sit motionless in his armchair, facing the mirror on his wardrobe, always wearing his overcoat. His umbrella was invariably close by and he would use it to lean on whenever he tried to move. Poor Satie! The slightest effort tired him. He had even invented a whole system of strings which enabled him to turn the lights on and off and to open the door without having to leave his chair. Overcoming his distaste for the telephone, he would call his friends, but it would irritate him terribly whenever the exchange became too eccentric.[6]

He moved to another hotel, to be closer to his friends in Montparnasse. But his health deteriorated and he had to be taken to the Hôpital St. Joseph. He lingered on for several months and was admirably courageous. His increased sensitivity, along with his sense of physical decline, caused him to have terrible fits of anger. Yet to the very end he had moments of great delight. He was overjoyed at the presents his friends would bring and would have them placed in front of him, where he could look at them. He grew increasingly obsessed with order and systematic classification and his stubbornness never left him. He refused to see those who had abandoned him or who had not remained faithful to him. One of them had once entitled his critique of "Relâche" "Farewell Satie." "I cannot see them again, after all that," he said.

How should his strange conversion, of which Catholic writers have made so much, be interpreted? He received Communion and had a few long conversations with a priest, but we shall never know whether he

[6] From an address by Darius Milhaud on the occasion of the placing of a tablet at Satie's house in Arcueil.

was convinced. Was he touched by the grace of God? Did he want to make happy the nuns who had been "so nice" to him? There is really no point in speculating at length, since any hypothesis may be true.

Life left him gradually, day by day. On the 1st of July 1925 died "a very unassuming man, very bizarre, very sensitive, very amusing, very kind, who lay dying for four months under our grieved eyes, without ever quite ceasing to smile."[7]

[7] These lines are taken from a touching article written by Yves Dautun; he and Robert Caby were two young musicians whom Satie hardly knew but who showed an admirable devotion to the musician during his illness.

1, 2
3

M

*Monsieur & Madame
Alfred Satie ont l'honneur de
de vous faire part de la naissance
de Monsieur Eric-Alfred-
Leslie Satie, leur Fils.*

—

Honfleur, le 17 Mai 1866.

4, 5

7
6, 8

10, 12
11

13
14

15, 16
17

18, 19

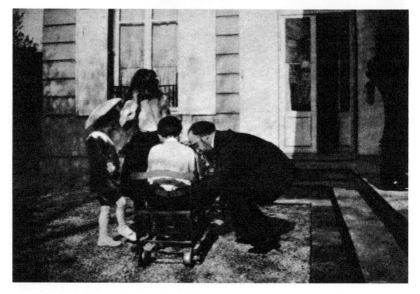

20
21, 22
23

24

25
26
27, 28

2

The Man

When you first start listening to him, all he says seems utterly grotesque. You catch glimpses of his thoughts only through a cloud of vulgar words and expressions, which clothe him like the skin of an impertinent satyr. He speaks only of armor-plated donkeys, of blacksmiths, of shoemakers, of curriers; and he seems always to be repeating the same thing in different words, so that ignorant men are tempted to laugh at him. But take the trouble to unfold his words, penetrate their inner meaning; then you will come to believe that they alone have meaning—you will find them all to be divine, containing the most noble images of virtue and encompassing almost everything that one must have before his eyes if he wishes to become an accomplished man.

These words are about Satie's "Socrate," but they could well apply to Satie himself. He too was much like the satyr Marsyas: a short, graying goatee; rather thick lips, twisted into a teasing smile which could at times be cruel; a sensual, greedy nose. The expression of his eyes, hidden behind a pince-nez, could change at a moment's notice from gentle to teasing to furious. "To know him, one had to see him without his glasses. Even then, the irony would remain; but let it disappear for a moment and you would receive the caress of those gentle, nearsighted eyes in whose light appeared at last the real Satie."[1] His face, crowned by a strangely pointed skull, was quite beautiful, enigmatic and ever-changing. In his "Memoirs of an Amnesiac," Satie provided a description of himself dating back to the year in which he joined the army as a volunteer: "Dark brown hair and eyebrows; gray eyes (probably flecked); stormy brow; long nose, average mouth, wide chin, oval face. Height: 5'6"." His dress was conventional: he often wore a dark gray jacket and a black coat with collar turned up. With his umbrella and bowler hat, he resembled a quiet school teacher. Although a Bohemian, he looked very digni-fied, almost ceremonious. A soft, deep voice, unhurriedly familiar and friendly, trans-formed his words into mysterious confi-dences. He was seized by unexpected bursts of laughter, which he would stifle with his hand. He walked slowly, taking small steps, his umbrella held tight under his arm. When talking he would stop, bend one knee a little, adjust his pince-nez and place his fist on his hip. Then he would take off once more, with small, deliberate steps. None of his friends could keep up with him on his long nightly walks. He hated the sun—and yet, is not his music full of sunshine? "What a bore this sun is; what a nuisance! It looks like a huge calf with a head as red as a cock's. It should be ashamed of itself!" He was not afraid of the rain; he had his umbrella. His odd character, his fits

[1] Maxime Jacob, *Vigile*.

of melancholy, drove him out of doors in the most terrible weather. At Verrières, during a certain period of Satie's life, the owner of a wine shop would always say to his wife, whenever the weather looked bad: "Today, it will rain all day; doubtless we shall see the gentleman of Arcueil." At noon, Satie would appear under his umbrella.

With the mood I'm in, don't come to me to talk about reason.
L.-P. Fargue

His conversation was extremely entertaining. Very talkative, he would watch the person to whom he was speaking, through the corner of his eye, judging the effect of his jokes. In the company of a few close friends, he would be truly delightful. Smoking innumerable cigars, he would discourse at great length on any subject with extraordinary lucidity; his manner would become less affected and he would often appear gentle, compassionate.

He spoke with great subtlety on all subjects other than his art—of which he spoke as little as possible, especially with musicians. At times, a baroque erudition would add, with an ironically elevated tone, a comic note to this endless flow of words. He would cross and uncross his legs, mutter "Quite so, quite so" or "Could be, after all" and guffaw into his beard. On social occasions, he was very polite, very charming. Whenever his wealthy friends in the *Faubourg* invited him to dinner, he arrived, bowing affectedly and gravely, his manner excessively polite, but wholly unable to resist the temptation to whisper in the unbelieving ear of the lady sitting next to him his opinion on the Council of Arcueil or his belief that his Bolshevik sympathies compromised his musical success. He ended his lectures with "profound salutations" and claimed to be the obedient servant of his audiences. This whole attitude became unnerving whenever he felt that he was being flattered and given too much attention; the devil within him led him to unmitigated folly or to blatant unpleasantness or insolence. When some of his friends, not always sincere, tried to take advantage of him, he would explode. His fits of anger were terrible; the most expressive and the most undeserved insults would then pour forth. Such outbursts would be followed by quarrels that remained inexplicable to all but Satie. A mere trifle would cause him to become angry and disappear: a hole that Georges Auric made in an umbrella, a cherry pit thrown at him in fun by a child of an old aristocratic family to whom he gave lessons, were sufficient cause for such extreme reactions.

But his friends think that these apparently baseless quarrels had in fact a deeper cause: a free soul, he deliberately wanted to remain detached. Cocteau justly noted: "When Satie would pout, behaving toward me in the way which had caused most of his friendships to end, I would look into myself and find a bad weed which had been the first cause of his apparent capriciousness. As soon as I got rid of the weed, I would see Satie coming back to me."

Often he would quarrel with people for reasons involving his dignity. This need for conventionality and respect was indeed a curious paradox in Satie. Did he joke when he demanded—he, a Bohemian—that his friends treat him with proper respect? It is unlikely. His innocence is a better explanation for this curious behavior; children easily become indignant.

It is difficult to define clearly any one aspect of Satie's character, because of the strange contradictions that destroy any conclusion one may reach. Consider, for example, the neatness of his attire on the one hand, and the incredible state in which he would leave his room, on the other. After his death, his friends entered his room and were left speechless with astonishment. One of his two pianos was invisible, buried under an incredible pile of documents and newspapers. Satie never threw anything away, and it is difficult to tell where he slept in this sad abode cluttered with all his belongings. In one corner, dozens of shirt-collars; elsewhere, some new shirts that had never been worn. The "masterpieces" hanging on his walls were protected from the dust by tiny paper awnings:

To live among glorious works of art is one of the greatest joys that can be experienced. Among the precious monuments to human thought that my modest fortune made me choose to share my life with, I will speak of a magnificent False-Rembrandt, deeply and largely rendered, so good to feel with the tips of your eyes, like a fat fruit, too green.

And the old master would walk out of his property, of his "estate," fresh, clean, and tidy. It is understandable that he never brought his friends to his home. Not only was he dignified; he was also very proud.

To be able to lead this strange, nocturnal life, to bear all these deprivations, Satie must have been in extremely good health. He was indeed strong, well built, and very resilient. In his miserable little room, where gymnastic equipment was found after his death, he would exercise. Along with his good health came a fierce appetite. Though he drank abundantly, he ate even more:

Having a good appetite, I eat for myself, but with no egoism, no bestiality. In other words, I sit much better at the table than I do on horseback.

At meals, my role has its importance. I partake of food in the same way as audiences partake of theater.

Dishes that are the product of a calculated virtuousity, of a careful science, are not those that retain my "tasting" attention. In art, I prefer simplicity; the same is true for food. I applaud a well-cooked roast more enthusiastically than I do the subtle work of a piece of meat carefully dissimulated by the artful hands of a master of the sauce.

During the wild years of his youth, Satie had the reputation of being immoderate—but did he deserve it? He himself claimed that at the time when he accompanied Vincent Hyspa, the latter was obliged to lock him up to make sure that he would be in a state allowing him to play the piano in the evening. Did not the evil "Ouvreuse du Cirque d'Eté" write that Satie had been thrown out of the Chat-Noir by Salis because "he played so badly and drank so well"?

His days were often spent at the café, where

a great number of intellectuals do not disdain to be seen . . . thus forgetting all the circumspection that a respectable man owes to himself, and a bit to others . . . . As Alphonse Allais once said to me: "A thing like this can ruin your prospects for a respectable marriage."

I do not believe that the fact of going to the café or to any other place can be bad in itself; I confess to having done a great deal of work there, and I believe that the celebrities that have been there before me did not waste their time. The exchange of ideas that takes place can only be profitable, as long as one takes care not to attract attention. However, to prove my morality and to appear respectable, I say: "Young men, do not go to a café; heed the solemn voice of a man who has been there often—in his opinion—but who does not regret it, the monster!"

When I was young, I was told: "You'll see, when you're fifty." I am fifty and I haven't seen a thing.
Erik Satie

All his life, Satie remained a naive child; like Chrysaline, he was surprised by everything. His love of children was not a reasoned one. He was not a man interested in the funny things that children do and say, but an older brother who did not need to make an effort to join in their conversations.

Children love new things; it is only when they reach the age of reason that they lose this taste. They instinctively hate old ideas. They sense that it is these ideas that will bore them later, when they will be in possession of their "intelligence." . . . While he is still tiny, the child watches the man and knows him well. Believe me, it does not take him long to see what an oaf he has before him.

Up to the moment of his death, Satie experienced the enthusiasms, the disillusionments, the indignations of youth.

With the same sincerity he criticized his
landlord for demanding payment of his rent,
and a neighbor for boasting of his dishonest
activities. He discussed seriously and with
violent partisanship such diverse issues
as umbrellas, religious practices, extrem-
ist political parties, and Gothic calligraphy.[2]
"I came to this world very young, at a very
old time," he said. A few days before his
death he said to one of his disciples: "One
must be intransigent to the very end." Is that
not the language of naïveté? His youth, this
exceptional gift he had, allowed him continually to renew himself with unwavering
good fortune—and to die a very poor man.
We have seen how he took part in the children's games at the Arcueil *patronage*,
how he danced with them and how they
loved him. One day a child told him that he
was saving all his money in a piggy bank.
Satie was shocked and wished he could take
back the coins he had just given him! When
the children fought, he separated them and
consoled the weaker ones. The child that had
lost the battle would stand there, his nose
bleeding, while Satie explained to him with
a half-serious, half-joking expression that
his little friend had certainly not done this
on purpose. He loved animals quite as much;

[2] It is important to note the extreme care with which he
wrote his letters and his musical scores; every note,
every sign is drawn with surprising regularity and
character. He had developed this love for calligraphy
around 1890, while studying graphics of the Middle
Ages. He very naturally identified with the naive il-
luminators. In his inexplicable little drawings, he follows in the footsteps of Nicolas Flamel, who drew
countless inspirations "which he himself published on
the walls."

he was known to seize lizards out of children's grasping hands, setting the poor animals free and waiting for them to disappear safely before he went on his way.

The artist contains within himself the intellectual. The converse is seldom true. Leon-Paul Fargue

The general education of the young Satie had been neglected. His father's pedagogic ideas, the freedom he gave his son, and his instinctive distaste for all kinds of authority did not give Satie a wide, universal knowledge. But we must remember that at that age Satie read voraciously, spending entire nights with books. He had an excellent memory that faithfully retained all he read, including the apparently useless things he studied at the public library, such as liturgy and Gothic art. Thus he acquired a singular and fragmented erudition that greatly influenced his thought and his style. Later, he read very little other than Andersen and stories about animals, returning again and again to the same tales and the same pages. The profound and simple truth in Andersen's beautiful tales impressed him, and there are some mysterious parallels to be drawn between certain exquisitely childish tales by Andersen and some of the scores by the master of Arcueil.

Wit and laughter came naturally to him. In the commentaries to his piano pieces, he is a little tense and his humor is a disguise. But if you listen to his music or read his letters, you discover a delightful sense of fantasy which could have made a marvelous story-teller out of him. It is to be hoped that these letters will one day be published, along with the sometimes ir-

reverent or Rabelaisian notes that were
found in his room along the margins of
notebooks or on pieces of old envelope:

—Ask anyone. Everyone will tell you, even the
idiots.
—The musician is perhaps the most modest of
all animals, but he is also the proudest. It is
he who invented the sublime art of ruining
poetry.
—If I hesitate to say out loud what I think, it is
solely because I do not have a loud enough voice.
—I have always suggested that free public rides
be organized in the State's chariot; up until now
no one has heeded me.
—"Yes, sir, I fought in the Hundred Years' War,"
the venerable old man said to me. I confess that
this did not interest me at all.

The "Piège de Méduse" is certainly his
"literary" masterpiece, in which his wit, so
similar to that of Alphonse Allais, appears
most clearly. The names of Max Jacob and
Léon-Paul Fargue come to mind, after that of
Allais, if one tries to find poets whose
imagination at times resembles that of Satie.
Indeed, one could find many more similari-
ties between these three artists which have
not been given the attention they deserve.
Thus, if one recalls the last page of Fargue's
"Kriegspiel" one can relish the following
notation by Satie:

2 flutes "à piston" in F sharp
1 alto overcoat in C
1 spring-lock in E
2 slide clarinets in G minor
1 siphon in C
3 keyboard trombones in D minor
1 double bass of skin in C
1 chromatic tub in B
These instruments belong to the marvelous family

of the cephalophones, have a range of thirty octaves, and are absolutely unplayable. An amateur
in Vienna (Austria) once tried, in 1875, to play
the siphon in C; as the result of the execution of
a trill, the instrument burst, broke his spinal col-
umn and scalped him completely. Since then no
one has dared avail himself of the powerful re-
sources of the cephalophones, and the State has
been forced to forbid the teaching of these instruments in municipal schools.

Readers of the S.I.M. have not forgotten
the extraordinary "Memoirs of an Amnesiac," which appeared between 1911 and
1913. Later, his lectures and articles became
more solemn: they were written to defend a
cause or to attack it. Although they were still
occasionally enlivened by a charming sense
of humor, their functional character took
away some of their burlesque poetry.

This poetry, which is only apparent to
the musician who takes the trouble to look
more deeply into Satie's music, adds a
note of restrained lyricism to all of his work:
chords and melodic lines have the beauty
of rare epithets or of rich rhymes. Satie's
poetry is also to be found at times in the
commentaries to his piano pieces, which are
truly prose poems:

The swing:
It is my heart that swings to and fro. It isn't
dizzy at all. What tiny feet it has. Will it ever
come back to me?
March of the Great Staircase:
It is a big staircase, a very big one. It has more
than one thousand steps, all in ivory. It is very
beautiful. Nobody dares use it, for fear of spoiling
it. Even the King has never used it. To leave his
room, he jumps out of the window. And very
often he says: I love this stairway so dearly that

I shall have it stuffed. Wouldn't you feel that way too?[3]

Satie has often been spoken of in comparison with others. This may seem a paradox, but comparisons have been looked for all the more since it is in fact impossible to compare him with anyone. In describing an artist, critics like to be guided by an analogous personality; if this proves difficult, the critic forces himself until he comes up with a name and joyfully announces his discovery. Thus were mentioned the names of Henri Rousseau, Cézanne, Picasso, Mallarmé, Rimbaud and, in this book, Max Jacob and Fargue. But despite all the interpreters of his character, Satie is unique, both as a man and as an artist. One could even speak of several personalities, not only different, but even opposed—the Janus of music, as André Cœuroy finally noted.

This variety, these contradictions that make the study of Satie's personality so fascinating, were undoubtedly among the real causes of his failures and of the lack of understanding that he encountered. "Changing one's character" is not permitted—in France. The general public is not so fastidious concerning questions of dogma; it does not demand "iron-clad personalities." It is the critics—although they ought not to be guided by laziness—who will not accept the fact that an artist has to rejuvenate himself. If "Mercure" and "Relâche" did not meet with great success, it is not because these

The exercise of an art demands that we live in a state of the most absolute renunciation.
Erik Satie

---

[3] Are these lines not reminiscent of Andersen's "The Shepherd Girl and the Chimney Sweep"?

works are inferior, but because they were
overshadowed by "Socrate." In the minds of
"serious" people, Satie did not have the right
to "sully his hands" with these two ballets,
which appeared to them as a regression. To
forgive such ups and downs, they could only
have invoked the excuse of genius, which is
what they did in the case of Picasso and
Stravinsky. Satie, however, was considered
to be not an artist of genius but simply a
practical joker: "It is, alas, certain that I
have no taste, no talent whatsoever. I have
been told this often enough." An amateur,
self-educated, a poor fellow who had been
dragged out of his little attic but who could
not bear strong light. From time to time the
critics were obliged to recognize a successful piece of work, but they waited for him
around the corner and destroyed his next
piece because there was no "progress."

To be forever a beginner! Is that not the
most beautiful, the most disinterested
attitude? Certainly, Satie couldn't have cared
less about "making the grade"; and trying
as he did to escape others as well as himself,
he did not take the paths that would have led
to success. He used to ask: "What do you
prefer, music or groceries?" He decided for
music.

Those were troubled days! Mozart and
Bach did not have carping critics pouncing
on their scores to judge whether or not there
was any evidence of a progression in them,
to find out to what influences they had been
exposed. What would M. Pierre Lalo write if
a new Johann Sebastian were to compose
the "Coffee Cantata" after a "Passion"?

Today, every composer has his own language, certified and compulsory. It is a mark of real courage for a composer to sever himself from his style, but great energy and a beautiful contempt for success are necessary for this.

To capitulate will always be a sign of weakness, and even of cowardice . . . . A real musician must submit to his art; . . . he must place himself above human misery; he must draw his courage from himself and only from himself.

He was too dignified, too proud to accept compromise for success. In this he was helped by his limited concern for financial success, which was due less to contempt for money than to ignorance. His poverty only touched him when it became visible, when his clothes were a clear indication of it; but he soon learned to laugh about it. Whenever he had a little money, he would spend it rapidly to feed his friends, to buy collars and shirts. Then, he would not be able to buy himself a meal every day. "To me this meant no more than abstention in matters of food. There really wasn't anything to it."

Success escaped him in much the same way. To be sure, if one wishes to be fair, his triumph of the 'twenties influenced his personality; his attitude toward his interpreters became ferociously exacting. In a way, this was his vengeance. His contempt for easy success through compromise remained unbending to the very end. He made this very clear in 1924 when he broke away from those who did not hesitate "to prostrate themselves":

I have no dislike whatsoever for those who have "arrived." They have a feeling for movement that is far from unpleasant. Only, the goal that they wish to reach makes me wonder and worries me (very little, I may add). Yes . . . . Simply, I question myself politely, saying to myself: Where do they want to arrive??? What do they want to get to??? At what time? . . . . In what place? . . . . And I am troubled and fearful for them.

As for me, I have never been success-oriented and I hope that I never will be. Yet, I quite understand that others may wish to indulge in this special exercise, however amorphous and certainly cumbersome (for oneself) . . . . Yes . . . . For in forty years I have seen many a "success," and in my days they were just as shrewd as they are today.

Well, all—do you hear, all—have "arrived" . . . nowhere, and even less than nowhere. Although some have "arrived" in various academies and other places . . . infamous places . . . Yes.

"He must have been terribly lonely?" she ventured.
Andersen

J'étaus ici, tout seul avec mi. Faudraut voir m'figure triste. Personne ne pensau à mi, sauf vous et trois cents amis. J'arrivau l'soir à m'maison, toute vide. L'piano m'regardaut, l'pauvre fieu; il n's'avaut pas.
Erik Satie
(letter to Pierre Bertin)

Loneliness could in itself explain the strangeness of his personality. Notwithstanding his friends and comrades, whether in his retreat at Arcueil or in the cafés, he was always "reduced to isolation." Ever since his childhood he had been introspective and, in his way, a dreamer. "Man was made to dream as I was made to have a wooden leg," he said. The universe he had built for himself gave him unusual habits and odd ways which to some appeared charming, but which to others were a source of irritation. It is quite logical that he should have been condemned in the name of "reason." Those who knew him well knew that his alert mind was lucid and perfectly balanced. "The more of us musicians there are, the crazier we all become," he observed with his usual wit. We refer the reader to all that has been written about madness, genius, and so forth. In any event, no generalizations can ever be made; each case is a special one.

Solitude also explains the cruelty and intolerance which he sometimes showed. He was as nasty as a willful child, and his friends have cause to remember this. He was slow to forget his grudges; he was in fact as touchy as he was sensitive.

He did have some real friends, whom he adored. His faithfulness to Claude Debussy remained very real and beautiful for twenty-five years. Luis Laloy has very well described the ties that held the two musicians together:

A tempestuous and yet indissoluble friendship bound [Debussy] to Satie. Rather, it was like one of those family hatreds, exacerbated by the repeated shock of incompatible traits, and yet leaving intact the deep sympathy of the characters which was due to their common origin. They were like brothers who through the events of their existence found themselves in very different situations: the one rich, the other poor; the first friendly but proud of his superiority, ready to make it felt, the second unhappy beneath his playful façade, paying for his drink with jokes to amuse his host, hiding his humiliation; always ready to attack one another, yet unable to stop loving each other tenderly.

His comrades of Arcueil were never quite sure of the friendship he had for them; he seemed to be searching in their company for some simple environment. In truth, he probably preferred them to the world of music, which he did not like at all.

At various times he placed himself, with wonderful unselfishness, at the disposal of young people. He even helped those who

professed their commitment to esthetic
principles opposed to his own. "The artist
is free in his taste," he would say; "I would
never dare attack anyone who does not think
as I do." In defending these young artists,
he imposed on himself a sort of sacrifice,
separating himself forever from the musicians of his own generation. The "Six" of
the Arcueil School owe a great deal to this
mentor; some of them remember this, while
others deny it and attack him. Some indeed
acted in a despicable manner during the
last year of their "Master's" life.[4]

Women did not play an important part
in Satie's life. As a mature man, he was not
known to have had any affairs. His friends,
observing his immaculate collars and shirts,
thought that he had gained the favors of an
Arcueil laundress. But this was not true. To a
question put to him by Madame Conrad,
Satie he answered: "You wish to know why I
never married? Simply because of the fear of
being horribly cuckolded, I tell you. And I
would deserve it entirely: I am a man whom
women do not understand." Still, Robert
Caby has observed the gentleness with
which Satie evoked the feminine in such
works as "Poèmes d'amour," "Ludions,"
"Relâche." And one must not forget the delicate and profound notes of the "Valse
fuguée" in "Mercure."

---

[4] We have decided not to go here into the influence that
Satie had on the musicians of his generation and on
those who followed. It is too early for that, and space
limitations do not allow it. Let us simply remind the
reader of Cocteau's statement: "Satie indicates a new,
untouched road on which each is free to step and leave
his footprints as he pleases." (Le coq et l'arlequin.)

It is with a certain hesitation that we approach Satie's religious and political convictions. The "Divine presence" probably haunted him from the days of his youth; his natural mysticism, which was nurtured by the elevated feeling of his art and by vague superstitions about the devil, witchcraft, and magic, progressed from the Rosicrucians and his own "Church" to his strange death-bed conversion. He led his friends in Arcueil to believe in his deep faith, but he made fun with them of priests —whom he called "vobiscum"—and of the ceremonial. It has also been said, and probably rightly, that ritual pomp and the somewhat mysterious organizations attracted him greatly. Religious preoccupations also appear in his letters, but in an ironical tone that does not allow us to come to any firm conclusions about them.

As to his subversive political opinions, they are hardly credible. Nonconformist, hating the spirit of war and the bourgeoisie (with his personality, he could not have done otherwise), he gravitated toward parties with socialistic tendencies.[5] However, he knew absolutely nothing of Marxist doctrines; communism could not have appealed to him, for his individualistic spirit would not submerge itself so easily. But he loved to go to those smoky meetings, where he would savor the assorted militant loudmouths. Moreover, he adored the little scandals

[5] "Passing by a monument erected in the memory of the children of Tremblay-sur-Mauldre (S.-et-O.) who fell on the battlefield, Erik Satie said to me: 'What, is this *all* the dead they've got here?' with an inimitable tone, a smile impossible to describe." (Pierre de Massot)

that he caused among his wealthy friends when he spoke of his involvement in the Soviet of Arcueil.

Every morning, with a medium soft brush, clean your brain of all that it has eaten the previous day.
L.-P. Fargue

Much has been said about his intelligence, his extraordinary astuteness. His insight was such that it did him great harm on the esthetic level. But what does that matter if he drew from it the most noble satisfactions! The total image of the man can only be greater for this. When he had conceived and produced a work for which he adopted a new style, he would immediately perceive its drawbacks, its weak spots and deformations, as well as the processes by which his new idea would later be altered. This foresight may have prevented him from expressing himself more fully. Timidity thus sprang from an excess of intelligence. He was led to farce in order to disguise his thoughts, although disguise is not the right word since instinctive spontaneity is precisely one of the most alluring qualities of his music. It would be better to speak of belittlement of thought, to which must be added artistic uncertainty. Never satisfied with his achievements, he was always searching for something new; at the age of 55 he said to his friends: "If anyone were to find something really new, I would start again at the beginning." This is why he cherished very young, forward-looking musicians, brutally cutting himself loose from those who lived in the past, even when he loved them. It was a punishment to which he subjected himself in the name of his most intransigent principles.

33
34, 35

Hôtel du Baron Pulard
Construction tout en fonte

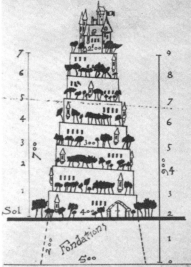

Église Métropolitaine d'Art de Jésus Conducteur.

Grands dignitaires:

Le Parcier — Robe rouge, capuce violet.

Le Grand définiteur
Le Grand prévôdent
Le Grand cloîtrier   } Robe rouge, capuce blanc
Le Grand prévôst

Les définiteurs 10 } Robe rouge, capuce gris

Dignitaires:

Les Prévôdents 25 } Robe violette, capuce rouge
Les Cloîtriers 50 } Robe violette, capuce blanc

Officiers claustraux:

Les Prévôts Blancs 200 } Robe blanche, capuce violet
Les Prévôts Gris 40,000 } Robe grise, capuce blanc

Chevaliers:

Les Prévôts Noirs profès 8,000,000 } Robe noire, capuce blanc
Les Prévôts noirs convers 1,500,000,000 } Robe noire, capuce gris.

Vêtement: Cotte de mailles à capuchon, à manches et à jambières; robe à capuce; heaume conique à nasal; et gants de mailles.

Armes: Une large épée de bataille et une lance longue de cinq mètres.

Tirage unique à 150 exemplaires.

Nº 1 à 50 sur papier de Hollande.

Exemplaire Nº 45 pour Erik Satie
musicien médiéval et doux, égaré dans
ce siècle pour la joie de son
bien amical

Claude Debussy

27 oct 92.

✝ Congrégation deſ Pauureſ cheualierſ
de la ſainte Cité,

Ordre religieux & militaire, inſtitué par de
pieux ſquelettes danſ le but de défendre la
chrétienté & de protéger leſ égliſeſ. Leſ Pauureſ
cheualierſ maintiennent la paix publique & la
religion & connaiſſent de touſ leſ crimeſ qui
peuuent troubler l'une ou l'autre. Leſ menbreſ
de cette congrégation ſ'enueloppent du myſtère
le pluſ profond & ont danſ toute l'Europe deſ
initiéſ qui leur défèrent leſ coupableſ. Rien n'eſt
épargné pour fauoriſer le déueloppement de
l'Ordre & pour l'attacher au Saint-Siège : le
nombre deſ congréganiſteſ ſ'accroît prodigieuſement;
cet ordre compte deſ centaineſ de maiſonſ; deſ
milliers de couuentſ ſont affiliéſ au monaſtère
principal. Leſ Pauureſ cheualierſ mènent une
uie trèſ auſtère; ilſ doiuent faire leſ troiſ uœux
monaſtiqueſ d'obéiſſance, de pauureté, de
chaſteté; ilſ renoncent à touſ leſ bienſ de ce monde
& uiuent d'aumôneſ; & ne peuuent payer
ni droit, ni tribut, ni péage : leurſ maiſonſ
ont droit d'aſile. Ilſ portent un habit blanc,

orné d'une ✝ double croix rouge. Le
chef de la congrégation a le nom de grand
maître; l'ordre ſe diuiſe grandſ prieuréſ, prieuréſ
& commanderieſ. La congrégation deſ Pauureſ
cheualierſ émane deſ Templierſ, deſ Sachetſ,
deſ Hoſpitalierſ de Sᵗ Laſare de Iéruſalem, deſ
Béguardſ, & de l'Egliſe ✝ Métropolitaine
d'Art de Iéſuſ conducteur. Leſ Pauureſ
cheualierſ ſont gardienſ du Sᵗ Sépulcre.

Le Parcier :

ERIK SATIE ✝

Cher Monsieur Satie, je me permets de prendre
la plume des mains vénérables de votre frère pour
la faire servir à mon usage personnel. Permettez
donc à un des membres les plus indignes de la
Chrétienté de porter la main à son chapeau et
de se présenter à vous sans la moindre pudeur.
La photographie ci incluse vous donnera l'aspect
physique de cet individu qui signe

Lépaqueľ

et vous salue.

Arcueil, le 14 du mois de Août de 99.

Monsieur Paillet,

Pourquoi nous attaquer à Dieu lui-même? Il est causé malheureux que nous pouvons l'être; depuis la mort de ton pauvre fils, il n'a goût à rien, mange du bout des dents.

Pour qu'il l'ait aidé à sa bonne mille diable; il est encore tout épaté que les hommes aient pu faire un aussi mauvais coup, vis-à-vis de celui qu'il chérissait; et il n'a de cesse que pour murmurer, dans le mode le plus triste: cela, ce n'est pas honnête!

Je doute qu'il arrive en ce monde, même un de ses sauveurs: les hommes l'ont dégoûté de faire voyager sa famille.

Laissons-le donc tranquille, Mes amis; prions-le sincèrement; comme nous devons le faire, du reste. C'est Moi, Saint Luk d'Arcueil, Parcier et Maître, qui vous le dis.

SAMEDI 7 AOUT 1909
à 8 heures 3/4 du soir
Dans les Salons de M. DOUAU
43, Rue Emile-Raspail, 43
ARCUEIL-CACHAN
Vin d'Honneur
Offert à M. SATIE
Par un groupe d'Amis
A l'occasion de sa nomination au grade
d'Officier d'Académie
Prix de la Carte : 1 Fr.
Enfants au-dessous
de 12 ans : 0.50

Arcueil, le 14 janvier 1911

Mon bon Pouillet —
    Voici un programme des "Jeunes".
    Tu y verras une notice — très incomplète —
Sur ton vieux frère.
    Comment vas-tu ?
    Ravel est un prix de Rome d'un très
grand talent.   Un Debussy plus épatant.
    Il me certifie — toutes les fois que je le rencontre —
qu'il me doit beaucoup.
    Moi, je veux bien.
        Ton frère :
P-S. Tu as reçu ma lettre du 10 ?

42
43

Notre principe commercial: faire du neuf avec du vieux.

— Nos morceaux sont garantis
sans quintes ni octaves.

Petit luthier.
La maison se charge des réparations
harmoniques.

Les compositeurs de la maison
n'emploient que de vieilles harmonies
éprouvées par un long usage.

Au Goût ~~d'autrefois~~ d'aujourd'hui.
Toute notre musique moderne a été
soigneusement retouchée par nos
employés.
Spécialité de remaniement de
musique.

Les clients sont prévenus que nous
venons d'acheter un grand choix de
symphonies. Ces symphonies, revues et
corrigées dans nos ateliers, seront mises
~~vendues~~ au point pour les besoins de notre
importante clientèle.
Soucieuse de contenter tout le
monde, la maison prend toutes les
observations et y fait droit de suite.
—— Une symphonie? Voilà, madame.
—— Elle n'a pas l'air très amusant.
—— Nous pouvons vous la donner arrangée
en valse, et avec paroles. Elle est jouée dans
tous les cafés.

Etude pour un buste
de M. ERIK SATIE
peinte par lui-même,
avec une pensée :
Je suis venu au monde
très jeune dans un temps
très vieux.

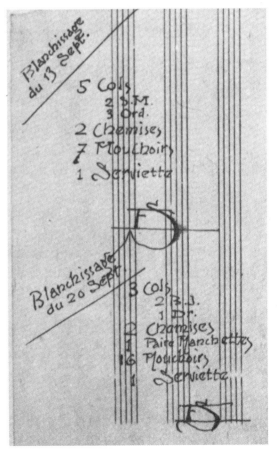

Arcueil-Cachan
27 juillet 1918

Cher Gros Ami — Je viens d'être très malade. Le médecin pleurait auprès de ma couche. Il disait : — « Il va mourir! « Je n'y suis rien ».

— Oui, Cher Gros ami, j'ai failli mourir moi-même. Votre ingénieur-aumônier en était la cause, le pauvre! Oui, je le jure.

Mon médecin — un herboriste savant — m'a cru perdu & m'a fait chercher par un chien de chasse.

Je suis retrouvé.

En lisant votre mot, je me mis à rire & manquai de m'étrangler avec le parapluie que creva Auric. Mais, ce n'est rien.

Bonsoir & bonjou.

Arcueil-Cachan
27 juillet 1918

Bonne Dadame si jolie ⚊ J'ai fait la connaissance d'un américain qui est évêque-lampiste de l'armée de son pays.

Il m'a dit : — « J'aime beaucoup « La Dadame; la Demoiselle-Sœur & le bon « Berlin. Ce sont des gens exquis, je « trouve ».

Il a raison — & comme évêque, & comme lampiste

Comment va? Revenez bientôt. Revenez dans.... dix minutes.

Paris est gai. Je m'amuse comme un tout jeune homme. Je vais au bal, avec ma femme & mes enfants. Je danse toutes les fugues de Bach. Revenez.

Bien à vous.

50
51, 52

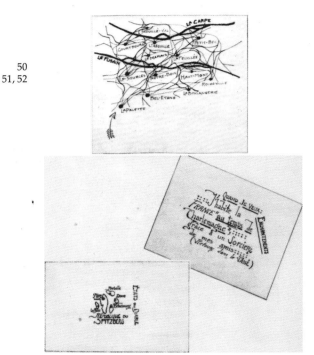

.... en rentrant chez moi, j'y trouvai un riche trousseau ;... & un somptueux mobilier remplaçait l'ancien. .... Sur une table, je vis un carnet de chèques inépuisable .... Un vieux domestique se tenait à mes ordres ...

Orchestre méchant DE TJORNDERÏË :

7 Flutes doublé (peurs.)
4 Tympanoni (hallucination)
8 Accordéoni (oppression)
5 Contrebasse (angoisse)

(Docteur Hulot)
ARMÉES MÉCANIQUES
de l'Enchanteur CARABUS
au service du Prince
JOSEPH ~ NAPOLÉON
BONAPARTE
descendant du faux roi de
ROME.

Tout en fonte XIII e s.
MAGIE
Caves; Salle; & Chambres; Greniers; & Cellule.
Cuisine; & Cabinet; & Grenier.
Terrain boisé
Ruelle en Tours-Basses
Faux Château

Un Conquérant: ......
.... De temps en temps y-
CŒUR-DE-VACHE "désolé"
un "coin" du Monde , ... &
disparaît ..... Est-ce le .....
DIABLE ? ...

Faux VIEIL VARCUEIL (Inconnu)
ENG. DT
COUR
NIMEZ.SUC.20.TO3
RUELLE-AU-DIABLE
PLACE
NOTRE-DAME.
NOTRE-DAME
Tout en Fonte (XIII e s.) MAGIE
A un Sorcier Brocanteur.

Le Sorcier acquéreur mystérieux
des Territoires* de Bagneux, d'Arcueil-Cachan,
de Gentilly-Bicêtre, de Villejuif, & de Chevilly.

Un Despote Invisible & Secret

1839-78

* Et influence sur ceux de Montrouge & Darnétal.

Plus les 2/3 du territoire de Rouen & tout celui
de Fécamp et leurs banlieues & voisinage.

BRUTES DE
GUERRE, hordes
de faux patriotes,
pillards, assassins
& traîtres. Bandes
terribles.

ARMÉES DE
TERRE & DE MER
du Dr X***
Ridicule chose
(Sorcellerie
comique)
LA TERREUR PAR
LE COCASSE.

Grandeur de Tous
Anarchie despotique
République puis
EMPIRE du TRAVAIL

France, Iles Britanniques, Belgique
& Hollande, Germanie, Helvétie,
le Nord de l'Italie, péninsule Hispanique,
le Canada, l'Afrique septentrionale
la Syrie & l'Asie-Mineure, Chypre,
Malte, l'Arabie & la Perse.

ASSERVISSEMENT LIBÉRAL
Résignation volontaire du Peuple

République
du Peuple
Empire du Peuple

(EXCURSIONS POLAIRES)
GRAND CINQ-MATS
« VOLAGE »

« L'invisible »
Grand transaérien
du Dr FAILLON — Sorciers

« St JEAN »
en acier
Grand Planeur acier

DIRIGEABLE
en cuivre
« LE SAUMON »

COMITÉ IMPÉRIALO CALOTIN

VOTEZ TOUS
pour le

A bas les Bouffeurs de Curés !
à bas les Sans-Culottes !
Rengainez vos gueules !
à la porte, les voyous !
Vive la Calotte !
Vivent les Officemards !

CANDIDAT BADINGUEUSARD GOUPILLONNEUR
Assez de Menteurs comme ça !!
ENLEVEZ LE GOUVERNEMENT DES
GOURDES ET DES POIRES !!!

Vendredi

Mon Cher Ami —— Je suis un
vieux bolcheviste & ne puis être des
vôtres. Je vous aime quand même,
et j'espère que nous ne serons pas
fâchés pour cela.
Bien à vous. Erik Satie

Erik SATIE
Compositeur de Musique

Voulez vous, cher ami, venir prendre
un punch ou un grog bien chaud?
Je suis chez Tulard
Vous venez?

Satie
1916
Jean 1916

3

His Works[1]

Prior to the Schola Cantorum (1885–1903)

1885

1886

"Valse ballet" and "Fantaisie valse" are agreeable compositions of a young man with fresh melodic ideas; their cadence already has the monotonous gentleness so appealing in Satie's early compositions.

The melodies published at this time by Alfred Satie are full of a calm, resigned melancholy. The writing is vague and subdued, like that which later was to characterize the impressionists, offering grave and naive laments with gentle harmonic progressions, notably unresolved ninths. It was a "Puvis de Chavannes" atmosphere, in which the gentle, twenty-year-old musician so delighted. The "Ogives" are series of perfect chords on modal themes, in honor of the Gothic style and the celestial gravity of the accompanying plain song.

The three "Sarabandes" remain fresh today. Although they are primarily interest-

---

[1] Unfortunately space does not permit us to develop this listing in greater detail. We can only encourage the musical reader to make his judgments by referring to the works themselves. In this, the following commentary may be of some use to him.

ing from a technical standpoint, they con-
tain enough music to be enjoyed also by the
layman. Delicate, refined, and profound,   1887
they are the mark of a musical "being".
As regards the harmonic idiom, we refer the
interested reader to several measures in the
first page of the "Roi malgré lui,"[2] which
was presented four months before the
"Sarabandes" were composed. This in no
way detracts from the melancholy of the first
two "Sarabandes" or the grace of the third.

The three "Gymnopédies" are a mir-
acle of intuition; a sad melodic line is   1888
sketched over a rhythmic background of
delicately dissonant chords. Debussy found
these works so outstanding that around 1895
he orchestrated two of them. In this new
form, they are played everywhere except in
France, and are recognized as being among
the most perfect works of the French school.
Such perfection clearly was no source of joy
to those who had only technique; they
termed them "trivial aberrations." And how
could they possibly appreciate music that is
"never finished," as Debussy said of
Moussorgsky?

In the three "Gnossiennes," the basic
cadence is more firmly established than it   1890
was in the "Gymnopédies." These pieces
too, with their Lydian scales and rather
oriental charm, have retained all of their
youth and vigor. Twenty-five years later,
writing for the S.I.M., Satie was to make fun
of himself for the insistent rhythm which
characterized a number of his earlier works,

---

[2] By Emmanuel Chabrier (Translators' note).

and to describe himself pejoratively as a "phonometrographer."

I believe I can state that phonology is superior to music. It is more varied. The monetary return is higher. To it I owe my wealth.

In any case, with the help of a motodynamophone, a barely experienced phonometrist can easily transcribe more sounds than the most capable musician could in the same lapse of time, with the same effort. It is thanks to this that I have written so much.

It is in the "Gnossiennes" that we find for the first time humorous indications written in over the notes, a device intended to unsettle the faithful and to force them to unmask the music. In this case, moreover, they had a profound meaning.

Satie's three Preludes to Peladan's "fils des étoiles" are written in an idiom entirely "invented" by their composer. With a certain clumsiness, but with a very sure musical sense, he piles up fourths, ties in very unusual chords, and ends up with a "courageously easy and complacently solitary" score, possessing a real "decorative" value. This new esthetic is briefly but very clearly summarized in an indication appearing in the first Prelude: "In white and motionless." This could equally well describe the "Sonneries de la Rose + Croix," where medieval themes delicately outline the dull hues of quiet and consonant chords.

The "Prélude de la porte héroïque du ciel," certainly the most perfect of his religious compositions, finds his mysticism at its most pure and most "musical." The harmonic idiom is no less original than that of the earlier compositions, but it appears to

1891

1892

1894

be more skillfully constructed. All these
early works, full of the most charming innovations, were made of harmonies which,
to quote Charles Koechlin, were "a little
bulky . . . . The successions of chords are
marked by a certain tentativeness, similar
to that of a primitive who has discovered a
new world all by himself." Only those pieces
that he allowed to be published in 1912 are
exempt from this description. It is difficult,
however, to blame Darius Milhaud for having put into the publisher's hands the
"Messe des pauvres," in which we find real
gems—the "Kyrie," "Prière des orgues,"   1895
and "Commune qui mundi nefas"—as well
as the phrase "s'appliquer au renoncement,"
which always guided Satie in his art.[3]

After a silence of two years, Satie composed "Pièces froides" ("Airs à faire fuir,"   1897
"Danses de travers"), which were free of
timidity and clumsiness: he had decided to
stop composing "on his knees." In his old
age, he said to Benoist-Méchin: "It is doubtless because you are still young that your
music is a little sad." In these pieces, cheer-
fulness and humor lightened his music.
Although technically the "Airs à faire fuir"
are not very different from the "Gnossiennes," the rhythms are livelier, the chords
are broken down, and the texture is more
fluid. The "Danses de travers" may remind
us a little of Fauré; but there is nothing
strange in this, for their fluidity and their
pure charm correspond perfectly to the

[3] "Quatre Préludes" and "Danses gothiques" (1893),
published in 1929, complete the list of compositions
of Satie's "mystical" period.

definition given by Fauré of French music in his preface to Jean Aubry's book. Moreover, the Niedermeyer school had been a stage in both composers' development.

The second of the "Airs à faire fuir," with its lively, cheerful theme and its skillful modulations, anticipates the exquisite "Jack-in-the-box." "Jack" is delightfully sprightly and fresh, containing melodic themes and harmonies that remain simple without a trace of banality. Written in gigue rhythm, it was orchestrated by Milhaud and produced by Diaghilev's ballet company in 1926, with lovely costumes and décor by Derain.

Satie claimed he had lost "Jack" on a bus. After his death, the manuscript was found behind one of his pianos, along with that of "Geneviève de Brabant," which was probably composed during the same period. "Geneviève," a miniature opera for marionettes with libretto by Contamine de Latour, is pervaded by indescribable freshness and naivete. Geneviève's two tender and delicate arias; the choruses, with their slightly popular tone; Golo's fearless aria; and especially the astonishing "Entrée des Soldats," which recurs like the "Promenade" in "Pictures at an Exhibition": all are gems —small gems to be sure, but charming. The flat colors, the laments, the simplicity of the opera, recreate the ancient romance of Geneviève and evoke the atmosphere of an Epinal engraving.

Satie's brief career at the *café-concert* certainly influenced his music, making it lighter and gayer. His waltzes and "inter-

1899

1903

mezzo américains" are not the only examples of this. One need only glance through the "Trois morceaux en forme de poire" to observe it. The full title of this work in seven parts, originally written for piano duet, is:

3 Morceaux en forme de Poire
à 4 mains
avec une Manière de Commencement,
une Prolongation du même,
et un En Plus,
suivi d'une Redite.

None of Satie's other works of this first period are as totally successful. Everything is present here: deep sadness (No. 1), rhythmic languor ("Manière de commencement"—"En plus"), jovial gaiety (No. 2), smiling melancholy ("Redite"), and power which, in No. 3, already anticipates "Parade." Few compositions for four hands give greater satisfaction to the performers; one that comes to mind is Gabriel Fauré's "Dolly."[4]

During his three years at the Schola Cantorum, Satie was a docile, hardworking student. From this period, we have today only two piano pieces, "Prélude en tapisserie" and "Passacaille." In them, we observe his budding passion for counterpoint, which was already reaching the lively precision of his later works, and for rigid form. The bass lines were becoming agile and lyrical.

1906

His first composition on leaving the

**Fugues and wit
(1908–1916)**

4 A curious similarity may be noted to No. 4 of the "Bilder aus dem Osten" by Schumann, originally composed for piano duet.

Schola was published under the title of "Aperçus désagréables"; it consisted of a Chorale and a Fugue composed in 1908, to which Satie added a Pastorale in 1912. Here he used counterpoint with great skill. The Fugue, with its complex and continually modulating theme, is very interesting; but one can wonder whether its severe chromaticity is not in fact an excellent joke—the spirited liberties he takes with the score would lead one to think so. In "En habit de cheval," the composer's intention is more purely musical; and he creates an exquisite sense of melancholy. Originally planned for full orchestra, "En habit de cheval" includes a section—the "Paper Fugue"— which illustrates Satie's idea of a modern fugue.

Although these works were very successful, Satie's nature and his sense of humor were such that he could not be content with such severe forms for long. Later, he composed more chorals and some fugues, but only in order to give a solid base to his inspiration—or simply to have fun.

This is when he decided to make use of his training in counterpoint in a manner not only personal but also totally new, allowing him to give free rein to his wit. We have already spoken at some length about his complex sense of humor, and there is no better word to describe the extraordinary fantasy which permeates the piano works published after 1912.

These pieces have often been criticized for their brevity. Doubtless, Satie's critics viewed his compositions in relation to the

1911

never-ending and repetitive sonatas and symphonic poems of earlier eras. Yet in truth, did Schumann not write pieces no longer than any of the "Préludes flasques"? As Koechlin justly noted, "development is not an aim in itself; it is a means and one that does not fit all works." In Satie's words: "The artist does not have the right to dispose uselessly of his audience's time."

The novelty of "Trois préludes flasques (pour un chien)" ["Three Flabby Preludes (for a dog)"] came as a charming surprise. Yet Satie's imagination is still kept in check here. "Sévère réprimande," a lively and emphatic toccata with singing bass chords; "Seul à la maison," a delightful two-part invention; "On joue," with lightly bouncing fourths and fifths and minor sevenths climbing menacingly up the keyboard: no trace of humor here, in the music. But the directions, in mock Latin, read "corpulentus, cœremoniosus, substantialis . . ." .

1912

"Sur une lanterne," admirably delicate and discreet, is perhaps the best of the "Descriptions automatiques." Sad chords over which is traced a hesitant melody, notes repeated and then vanishing; then suddenly, light, expressed by lively and bright harmonies. This is the first example of a new form of mysticism in Satie—a kind of elusive mystery, subtly evoked in a musical atmosphere which is partly poetic, partly amused, but very moving. Here popular themes also appear for the first time. Thus, in "Sur un vaisseau," the popular theme "Maman, les petits bateaux" is evoked. This idea, seemingly so un-

1913

sophisticated, is developed with surprising skill and great respect for the music; the themes do not appear at the outset, but seem to flow naturally out of the opening notes. "Sur une lanterne" is an excellent example of this.

The "Embryons desséchés" is written in brilliant style, with grandiose harmonies. The Holothuries, imaginary crustaceans invented by Satie, proclaim "It's so good to be alive," to a musical background where one can almost see "sunshine reflected in the puddles:"[5] the atmosphere is created very accurately in a few notes. The Podophtalma, other imaginary crustaceans, are described as they go out to hunt, scampering over the keyboard, paying no heed to the injunction "don't rush like that." They play a majestic air on the horn and set forth once more, only to be "forced by the author" into a final cadence ("cadence obligée de l'Auteur").

Each one of these musical gems should be analyzed separately. "Croquis et agaceries d'un gros bonhomme en bois" includes a lightly inflected "Danse maigre" and an "Españaña," which pays homage to Chabrier and pokes gentle fun at Debussy and his Spanish moods. "Chapitres tournés en tous sens" contains "Celle qui parle trop," the wife who talks too much, causing her unfortunate husband to die of exhaustion; "Le porteur de grosses pierres," carrying his rocks to the accompaniment of tired, dragging chords; and the lovely "Regrets des enfermés," where with another wry smile at

[5] Charles Koechlin.

Debussy, who had used this theme so ef-
fectively, Satie introduces the well-known
"Nous n'irons plus au bois." In "Vieux
sequins et vieilles cuirasses," Satie orients   1914
his music toward more gentle chords and
"prettier" things, particularly in "Chez
le marchand d'Or" and "Défaite des Cim-
bres". In "Heures séculaires et instantanées,"[6] the counterpoint becomes more
complex and perhaps a little too descriptive
for this author's taste; doubtless, this was
meant as a joke—in any case, it does not
make these pieces any less beautiful. The
"Trois valses du précieux dégoûté," often
frankly bitonal, seem to be making fun of
his old friend Maurice Ravel. Finally, in the
adorable "Avant-dernières pensées," dedi-   1915
cated to Debussy, Paul Dukas, and Albert
Roussel, Satie allows his poetic sense to
appear, while at the same time clarifying his
musical thought. This was the last of the
series; did he wish to indicate by its title,
dedication, and style[7] that he was about to
"shed his skin" once more?

Among the works of this important
period of Satie's life, two sets of pieces
appear particularly noteworthy: "Enfan-   1913
tines" and "Sports et divertissements."
The former, which were written for small

---

[6] In a preface to "Heures séculaires," Satie restricted the
use of the humorous commentaries which accompany
his music by warning "whosoever" might be tempted
to do so that he "forbids the text to be read out loud
during the performance of the music. Failure to conform with these instructions will cause the transgressor
to incur my just indignation. No special exceptions
will be granted."

[7] The style is bitonal, skillfully moderated by an unchanging theme to which the ear grows accustomed.

hands and are extraordinarily varied, include "Menus propos enfantins," "Enfantillages pittoresques" and "Peccadilles importunes." Using only five notes, he manages to recreate the spirit of children playing soldiers ("Marche du grand escalier," "Chant guerrier du Roi des haricots"), getting angry at each other ("Valse du chocolat aux amandes"), or quietly going to sleep . . . The kingdom of childhood was open to him; these images are very different from Claude Debussy's tribute to his dear little "Chouchou," which is the work of a grown man. They may be linked, because of their inspiration, to the "Album à la jeunesse." This is not music about children, or for children, but of a child.

1914

Darius Milhaud considers "Sports et divertissements" to be one of the most characteristic works of the French School. In any case, it is certainly one of Satie's best, consisting of twenty brief and perfect musical sketches, into which are compressed not only Satie's spirit but also that of French music, all of it prodigiously alive. Charles Koechlin has compared "Sports et divertissements" to Japanese engravings, noting their delicate precision and beautiful colors. Of course one cannot speak here of pure music, but rather of a perfect correspondence between the music and the commentary. It is the manner in which these subjects are dealt with that is pure: there is never a vague or imprecise line, but always a sensitive and faithful portrait. Again, each of these works should be dealt with independently: the "Choral inappétissant," marked "rébarbatif et hargneux" and dedicated to "those who do not love me"; "La balançoire," touching in its simplicity; the ironical "Chasse"; the grandiloquent "Comédie italienne"; the elegant "Colin-Maillard"; the exquisitely precise "La pêche"; "Carnaval," which ends on a questioning chord; "Le golf," marked "exalté"; "Le pieuvre," choking on a crab; "Water-Chute" and its uneasy hero; "Le traîneau," with its icy theme; the silly melody of "Le flirt"; "Feu d'artifice," its chords full of wonder.[8]

Parade

1916

Drums, clappers, tambourines, side-drums, treble siren, bass siren, typewriters, revolvers, lottery wheels, pipes, tom-tom, cymbals, xylophone, bottlephone, triangle. Was this "Parade"? Satie explained with apparent modesty: "I have composed a background to certain noises that Cocteau considers necessary to create the atmosphere of his characters." Did Cocteau really consider them necessary? At times he found them somewhat cumbersome. Besides, it is difficult to identify each author's contribution to a ballet, an art form which only finds its real meaning once it is complete. One can note in "Parade," however, a certain opposition between the music and the sets on the one hand, and the

[8] To this series must be added "Danses du Piège de Méduse," written in 1913 for small orchestra. This consists of seven brief, elliptic dances which have the same spirit, the same liveliness as "Sports." In them, the orchestra is extraordinarily lighthearted, and the music seems made for phonographic recording.

The following pieces should also be mentioned: "Choses vues à droite et à gauche," for piano and violin; a brief sketch (1913) to "Les pantins dansent," by Valentine de Saint-Point, and the gentle "Poèmes d'amour" (1914), for piano and voice.

subject matter on the other. The latter is the work of a poet, very compelling indeed, but the symbolic ramifications of which are seldom in harmony with the simplicity, the "cubism" of Jean Cocteau's collaborators. Satie's score could perhaps be described as "cubist" (without any analogy to cubist painting)—a reaction to the vagueness of impressionism—because it unfolds with an almost mechanical precision, moving with clockwork uniformity. It is an unadorned work, clearly delineated, conceived to serve as a "musical carpet" responding to the steps of the dancers. This humble conception of the role of ballet music notwithstanding, "Parade" is in its way a masterpiece. After the opening of the ballet, Igor Stravinsky said: "There are Bizet, Chabrier, Satie," meaning no doubt that Satie could easily achieve in his own music the deep and smiling simplicity of the prelude to Act II of "Carmen" or that of the "Joyeuse March." Moreover, "Parade" had the great merit of bringing the music hall into the world of "great" music, where it was to become a fertile source of inspiration for the younger generation of musicians. Actually, the idea had existed ever since "Petruchka," even though the actual execution of the two ballets was diametrically opposite. Where Stravinsky gave life to the crowd, Satie brings out the spirit of strolling players, a mixture of mechanical grace and masked sadness.

"Parade" opens with a choral (omitted in the piano arrangement), which leads into the "Prélude du rideau rouge"—a short, fugal exposition which is followed, as the curtain rises, by the entry of the First Manager ("Premier Manager"). The Managers' theme—with which Satie was quite satisfied, and this was seldom the case—is admirably evocative of the monotonous patter of the fairground. Truly an original theme, neither major nor minor, neither tonal nor atonal, it can be played either with three beats or with four. These two forceful pages, in which one can find all the signs of the objectivism that Stravinsky had made so very fashionable, are indicative of the careful work and great knowledge of the composer of "Parade," notwithstanding the apparent and deceptive simplicity of the score. The theme is presented four times, with an increasingly brutal accompaniment, the tonality of which is gradually affirmed; it then gradually gives way to two flutes and a horn, which introduce the Chinese Prestidigitator. The tempo of the music does not slacken, no oriental flavor is added: the score follows its course as regularly as ever. Over an insistent bass line, expressive melodies are quietly sung by the horns, then by a flute. There follows a brief passage, quivering and plaintive, then an ironic tom-tom (with the instructions "assume a false manner"), and the number ends as it had begun.

This classical ending is typical of "Parade." The entire work, as well as each individual part, is constructed symmetrically. The listener enters "Parade" through two gates, the fugue and the Managers' theme, through which he will pass again at the end of the work. This solid architecture is to be found in each of the three numbers.

The Second Manager then executes a silent dance without music and is followed by "The Little American Girl." Rapidly descending sixths lead to a bitonal, syncopated tutti. A swinging rhythm ("bend down carefully," instructs Satie) supports a fluid, singing theme. Then, after a page in which the hammerlike beat gradually subsides, giving way to the subtle voice of violins and the click-clack of a typewriter, a choral introduces the "Rag-Time du Paquebot." This is marked "triste" in the score, and a touching sadness in fact pervades it. The bass sings sorrowfully, the solemn chords of the brass resound powerfully. Yet the emotion and the power of the music stem solely from the combination of themes and chords, and no extramusical sentimentality intervenes to lower the tone of this section. The "Little American Girl" ends on a simple theme played by the woodwinds to a polyrhythmic background of strings and harp, following a passage in which a very strange scale "quivers."

The Third Manager "on horseback" introduces, once again silently, the last number: the Acrobats. The emotion here is less apparent: a rapid and regularly measured waltz, a pizzicato accentuated by the xylophone, mathematical syncopations. A slower page, in which a 16-foot bell drones, follows ("physionomique"); then the lively dance resumes.

The final dance of the Managers, "Suprême effort et chute des Managers," is accompanied by an orchestral tutti thundering out the theme that introduced them at the beginning. The Finale is comprised of pieces borrowed from three parts; Satie omitted this from the arrangement for piano in order to bring out better the construction of the whole. And the ballet is rounded off by the last eight bars of the fugue ("Suite au Prélude du rideau rouge"), culminating in an impressive cadence and a final resolution in C major.

The orchestration of "Parade" is simple and clearcut. It has that quality which Satie called musical transparency, one possessed by musicians whose music contains no "left-overs." The critics in 1917 accused Satie of not knowing how to orchestrate because his technique "lacked spice," grating against ears accustomed to impressionist vagueness. These orchestral sounds, which belong to him personally (they appear in the "Grimaces" composed 1919 for a production by Cocteau of "Midsummer Night's Dream"), are somewhat ingenuous and bring out his lively counterpoint extremely well.

"Parade" was truly a landmark in the history of theatre. It was revolutionary in every detail—scenery, costumes, choreography, and music—and had a profound impact on modern theatre:

It was indeed the genius of Diaghilev that led him to shed his old skin and turn to French art, grouping around himself the young painters and young musicians of Paris. . . . The truly great years for the Ballets Russes were during the period 1919–1924, encompassing both "Parade" and "Noces." (Boris de Schloezer)

As for the music itself, it has solidly

oriented the young French school of musicians toward clarity, toward pure music.

At the same time that he was working on "Parade," Satie composed three delightful melodies: "Daphénéo," "La statue de bronze," "Le chapelier." In these few pages he seems to have achieved the highest expression of humor and imaginative poetry. Through the purity of Satie's technique, the nocturnal calm of the close of "La statue de bronze" or the light counterpoint of "Daphénéo" reach a level of beauty devoid of all artifice or affectation to a degree which already foreshadows "Socrate."[9]

Socrate

In "Socrate" there is genius.
Charles Koechlin.

The first performance of "Socrate" met with laughter. "Strange, is it not?" was Satie's only comment. The critics, however, did more than laugh. Jean Marnold, not content, wrote:

At last, realizing that the joke had fallen flat, M. Satie has given birth to "Socrate," beating his great bass drum all the while. This "drame symphonique," as he calls it, consists of a rosary of brief phrases implacably reiterated, relentlessly calling forth faded and flagrant (?) memories of "Boris" and "Pelléas." All this serves as a background to Vicot Cousin's text, which is intoned like a drawing-room conversation. Impotence is too grand a word for so complete a nullity.

Jean Marnold had not understood; and he condemned his own judgment later in the same article, when he tried to find a

[9] "Sonatine bureaucratique," written in 1917, is a delicate homage to Clementi. Once more, Satie was here a forerunner; this "return to Clementi" is very evident, though not always successful, in the works of several musicians of the young school.

justification for the music of the "Six" as opposed to that of Satie:

As with all forms of art, including writing, musical beauty is objective and belongs to the realm of pure contemplation. In order to obtain adequate and commensurate enjoyment from a work of art, one needs to know it completely, to be impregnated with it to the marrow and to "contemplate" it only.

In speaking of "Socrate," it is impossible to say anything more pertinent and true. Georges Auric claims that Satie's music must be felt from the first moment. This may be true of his more "imaginative" works, in which his humorous eccentricities charm the listener or repel him from the start, but not of "Socrate."

"Socrate" is a difficult work; and its many beauties can seldom be appreciated on first hearing, except under particularly favorable conditions. The difficulty is not due to the extreme gravity or to the unusual harmonies of the music, which has been described by some of Satie's enemies as being simple to the point of indigence. Rather, its difficulty stems from its uniqueness. Nowhere at any time has anything comparable with "Socrate" been composed. But if originality in itself is not beauty, neither is tradition. Jean Cocteau said of Satie: "To please or to displease on purpose were to him incomprehensible attitudes. From the very beginning he adopted an untenable position." Thus, he was precisely taking on an untenable position when he composed a work that has no relation whatever with the music to which we are accustomed. Satie created a new universe for

himself into which it is impossible to penetrate without a period of apprenticeship.
So we must forgive those who understood
nothing: like Alcibiades, they reasoned by
analogy or by comparison. With his usual
penetration, Satie had foreseen this and had
published in the program notes for the
première a warning couched in terms that
appeared aggressive: "I request those who
do not understand to maintain an attitude
of complete submission, of complete
inferiority."

"I've made up my own libretto," he empha-
sized with malice; and his smile was meant
for his ex-collaborator, Cocteau. Satie probably feared Cocteau's too-great intelligence,
which would have led him to attempt some
acrobatic transposition of the original. The
"sauce coctique," as Satie would say in
moments of anger, cannot be served with
every dish. Going even a step further—
and this shows that Satie would not hesitate
to be cruel when he thought it useful—he
asked his friend René Chalupt to write a
brief preface to "Socrate."

He had been charmed by Plato's works.
No doubt he discovered analogies between
his own character and that of the old Greek
philosopher. Satie's humor is a sign of an
overdeveloped sensitivity. Through humor,
a form of intellectual suicide, he was able to
hide his misery and his sad destiny. He
would laugh for fear of becoming emotional;
and so would Socrates. The intuition that
guided Satie in the choice of the libretto
led those who analyzed him to compare the

two masters. Hasn't it even been found that the musician's work was also purely verbal? His music should not be taken into consideration, they said, it is of little interest; rather, one should look at his witty words, the naive advice of one who "professes injustice."

He was well aware of the difficulties of the task he had taken upon himself. He feared, and perhaps with some reason, that such a beautiful, timeless text might have no need for music. He did not wish to "add to the beauty of Plato's Dialogues," to add a pathetic note where it was unnecessary, to overemphasize pointlessly the brave simplicity of Death. Happily, he was able to achieve just what he wished: "an act of piety, an artist's reverie, a humble tribute." And he understood that his work would have to be "unprecedented," in no way comparable to anything else, so that it should never become old and outmoded. If it is not lost, this unobtrusive accompaniment will surely, a few centuries hence, be as "modern" as the text it illustrates.

The text, for which he chose perhaps unintentionally a dry and cold translation, he cut with skill, eliminating heavy or unnecessary words, as well as those whose particular emotional content would have restrained the flow of the work. In this way, he obtained three concise and complete fragments drawn from the Symposium, Phaedrus, and Phaedo, freely adapting Victor Cousin's text, without however adding a single word of his own.

The greatest quality of all of Satie's

work—this cannot be said too often—
is the precision of proportionality which
causes the music to be always in strict
step with the text which it embellishes or
to the subject matter in question. For
"Socrate" it was so difficult to enfold
in music such precise and terse prose that
the word genius comes to mind in the face of
his mastery. Since there is such perfect
conformity between libretto and music, it
is clearly necessary to love the former in
order to appreciate the latter. One must be
sensitive to fresh and motionless beauty
and to that "pure discussion" which so
many find boring. Some were unable to
enjoy it simply because it brought back
memories of their schooldays, when they
had pored over the pathetic narration of
Socrates' death.

To accompany Socrates in his philosophical wanderings, Satie could not but
choose simplicity and clarity. His own
modesty and humility where music was concerned led him in this direction. Since he
admired Plato's writings, he could not treat
them simply as a pretext for his own music.
His own role could not be dominant; on the
contrary, he had to submit, like a son to
his father, to the image he was framing. His
entirely objective score was meant to "fur-
nish" the philosopher's narrative. Moreover, his music had to be "Greek." Boris de
Schloezer's remark on this point is well
known: "There is nothing in common between Satie's music and Greek art, that is
neither reserved, nor modest, nor discreet."
But Schloezer added: "It is certainly not for

me to criticize Satie for creating a Socrates
of his own. Art is convention; and if I think
of Satie's Greece as resembling that in my
own imagination, then I conclude that the
music of "Socrate" is very Greek indeed.
Was it in order to Hellenize his score that
Satie used Greek—or, rather, Gregorian—
modes? I do not believe it. This would have
been a rather scholastic procedure, and
"professionalism" was a word he abhorred.
It is more likely that he was simply looking
for the rather timid, impersonal character
of ancient modes, which do not affirm as
they subtly vary and bewilder. Moreover, the
old scales attracted Satie through the infinite
possibilities of their archaic nature. They
allowed him to reach the smiling mysticism
of his earlier works, which in his heart he
lovingly nurtured.

The epithet "flaying technique," or strip-
ping away of all nonessentials, has evidently
done Satie an injustice. It was used by some
to describe that which is clear-cut, "to the
point." They referred to the surface instead
of penetrating to the skeleton, to the heart.
Some inferior impressionist works are not
"flayed"; they consist of skin only, without
bones. Like toy balloons, they can be
destroyed by a pinprick. Others believe that
the more notes in a chord, the better the
music. Intoxicated with oversonorous
harmonies, they remind one of those
painters who work with a trowel: from a
distance their paintings have some similarity
to reality, while at close range they are
nothing but relief maps. It was the same
critics who called Satie's works "trifles."

In 1919 the satanic Picasso burned his bridges, and his apparent return to Ingres amazed the artistic world. A clear echo of this event may be found in the preface to "Socrate": "He wanted his music to be simple and peaceful, modest in its nakedness . . . . This linear and precise design might have been the work of M. Ingres if Victor Cousin had asked him to illustrate these passages from Plato's Dialogues." This return to "linear" music, to melody, was hardly a new thing with Satie, dating back some fifteen years to the time, right after "Pelléas," when he had sensed that Debussy's style would only produce "the flamboyant, the exquisite, and the hairsplitting." In "Socrate" there is no inclination to asceticism as such, but simply the extreme economy that prevented him from adding a single note that was not essential. The simplicity of Satie's technique in this work is such that all analysis is difficult—or too easy. Simplicity takes on mystery when it engenders beauty, and it is no help to count the fifths, fourths, and sevenths that could easily reduce "Socrate" to merely an extremely monotonous recitative.

"Socrate" is a three-part symphonic drama with four soprano voices. The first two parts are presented as dialogues, while the third is a narration of Socrates' death. The vocal presentation is rhythmic, with no attempt at originality; and yet there is something absolutely unique about it. The syllables often have equal musical value, probably in order to emphasize the narrative quality that the performance is supposed to have; at first Satie had actually indicated "recitative (as if reading)" in the score. However, this bears little resemblance to the classical recitative, which is accented and dry; nor is it a symmetrically constructed melody. It is equally far from flowing melody in the Wagnerian manner and from the declamatory style of "Pelléas"; the vocal line is rather an extended but gentle lament, whose variety stems from its continuous changes of mode. Where key signatures become more precise, they are simple: two sharps or two flats, alternately major and minor. Octave intervals on which the voice lingers contribute to a feeling of quiet and serenity (see, for instance, page 40 of the score, "l'étrange chose, mes amis").

The orchestra follows its own path, independent of the singing. The themes appear again and again, sometimes in identical form, sometimes in a different register. These themes do not constitute a leitmotiv; rather, their repetition, regardless of the words they accompany, forms a solid base whose careful monotony increases the objectivity of the score.

The harmonies, generally consonant, are always unusual. Only occasionally does harshness follow from series of fourths and sevenths, naked intervals to which musicians are no longer accustomed, not having heard them for the past five or six centuries. This feeling of dryness, of "marble and steel," is more apparent in the piano version: the orchestra softens the sonorities considerably, particularly, as is the case in "Socrate," when a work is written in dis-

tinct parts situated at different levels of
pitch in the orchestra. Certain sections,
with their chords running in parallel,
demonstrate that here the Satie of "Socrate"
reverts to that of "La Porte héroïque du
ciel." But here the bass line is at all times
moving; only in rare cases does it become
immobilized by a pedal point. One could
dissect the entire technique used in "Socrate," but this would not prove a thing.
For, by his magic touch Satie was able to
rejuvenate the most hackneyed cadence, the
most decrepit refrain. The same goes for
chords (page 49) generally vulgarized by
organists. But one must penetrate deeply
into these syncopes, the three notes iterated
by the flute, then by the trumpet, and then
by the English horn—that voice which
"sings" so sweetly. I can only find one intentionally harsh passage, on page 67, where
through a cruel dissonance Satie creates
emotion: "Il nous fit voir que le corps se
glaçait et se raidissait" ("he showed us that
the body was becoming cold and rigid"):
a c sharp on the English horn against a c
natural on the violins.

The rhythm is not particularly varied; a
more varied rhythm would have meant de-
parting from the moderation which Satie
wished to observe. Each of the three parts
preserves its own rhythmic patterns. Thus,
"Les bords de l'Ilissus" is written in typi-
cally pastoral 6/8 time, given as

$$\text{♪ ♩ ♪ ♩ ♪ ♩ ♪ ♩} \text{ ,}$$

which imparts a great sense of lightness

to the orchestral background. In order to emphasize this feeling, Satie used a contrapuntal design whose two parts draw near and then apart, separated by a second, then by an octave, like wings that peacefully open and close. Over this background, the voice weaves its delicate web. Throughout this entire part there breathes an extraordinary poetry, a love of nature and of dreams. During the death scene, three principal rhythmic figures turn up: the 4/4 rhythm is at first given as

$$\text{♪} \,|\, \text{♩ ♩ ♩ ♪} \,|\, \text{♩ ♩ ♩ } \text{𝄽} \,| \quad ;$$

the eighth note marks a painful throe, but without overstatement. Farther on, the timpani and the double basses punctuate each measure thus:

$$|\, \text{♩ } \text{𝄾} \text{ ♪ ♩ } \text{𝄽} \,| \quad .$$

The ending is peaceful and serene; none of the measures is rhythmically subdivided.

The orchestration is reduced to the bare essentials: one flute, one oboe, one English horn, one clarinet, one bassoon, one French horn, one trumpet, one harp, kettledrums, and strings. The instruments are generally used in their middle registers. Two-part counterpoint is entrusted to the woodwinds, the scales are delineated by the strings, with an especially beautiful use of the violas. The harp doubles other parts and supports parallel chords. The horn and the trumpet create curious pedal points and do not have a very melodic role. Movements of great gentleness, where the counterpoint becomes more complex, are expressed by the strings alone. The kettledrums mark the rhythm; they have no trills.

This small, "linear" orchestra, "without spice" and so difficult to regulate, produces admirably measured and balanced effects. It is impossible to "explain" orchestral resonances, but these delightful gems (for instance, on page 22, "car l'eau est si belle, si claire, et si limpide") where the graceful melody is delicately sustained by the flute, the trumpet, and the violins, are indicative of the lovingness of the composer's inspiration.

The whole ending of the second part, Socrates' narrative by the sycamore, in this "charming place of repose," has an adorable freshness. The song, almost transcending the human voice, gently floats over the sevenths and the fourths of the strings with subtle balance (for instance, "goûte un peu l'air qu'on y respire . . . ; est-il rien de plus suave et de si délicieux . . . ."). The orchestral theme is interrupted, this break underlined by soft pedal points in the French horn, trumpet and cello. Then, the theme becomes treble—flute and violins—with a hesitant silence on the sixth beat of the measure. After some large and restful chords, it reappears, finally vanishing on an indeterminate chord (g, d, f sharp, and b).

For Socrates' death, Satie has found melodies touching "to the point of tears," as Henri Sauguet put it. Here, feeling is no longer disguised; and into these spellbinding moments, Satie has put all his sensitivity, all his heart. These phrases ("Dès que le froid gagnerait le coeur, alors Socrate nous quitterait . . . —Criton, nous devons un coq à Esculape, n'oublie pas d'acquitter cette dette . . . ".) have all the characteristics of the most authentic beauty. And the strange modulation of the last page, of such great simplicity . . . .

No words, no sincere praise can give an idea of the greatness of a work of art. "Well-meaning" musicians will recognize that the "Socrate" score has beauty, honest and simple beauty; but to love this work it is necessary that its intimate character, its loneliness, be maintained. Strong voices, large concert halls do not suit it at all. A singer who understands and who "sings" as little as possible, a friendly and trusting atmosphere—these are essential.

"Socrate" can then be an overwhelming revelation of a musical style that is neither grandiose nor refined, neither realistic nor vulgar, but simple and familiar.

After Socrate

1919

The five "Nocturnes" for piano are an affirmation of all that "Socrate" represents, with perhaps an even greater tendency toward objectivity. This is indeed, in five short pages, music in its pure state, impersonal combinations of sounds. The result is a rather intellectual musical pleasure, similar to that which can be experienced with Stravinsky's sonata. The "Nocturnes" are constructed according to a precise and unchanging plan: an air, a slightly more polyphonic central section, and a repetition of the first part. The main theme is set forth twice in the first part, the second time richly embellished. The great merit of the "Nocturnes" lies in their absolutely new accent, their completely new sounds, which create an "inhuman" musical emotion. Clearly, their conception and successful realization were a task of rare difficulty, as Satie himself conceded.

In writing the "Nocturnes," he may have had to force his inspiration a little. Did he feel that he was following the wrong path? Or did perhaps the genius his friends were attributing to him for such "serious" works scare him away? Whatever the reasons, "Trois petites pièces montées" marks a clear return to more natural and spontaneous music. Without stressing the third of the series, the instrumentation of which is intentionally humorous, we must here call attention to the pretense of heaviness in "Rêverie (de l'enfance de Pantagruel)," with its damped chords and its sleepy bassoon, and to the gay and familiar tone of the "Marche de Cocagne," with its trumpet counterpoint and its murmuring bass line. These three pieces form one of the best examples of the kind of "street-corner" music that Cocteau was talking about at the time: clear-cut, with precise orchestration and concise thought.

"La belle excentrique," a serious fantasy, is reminiscent of the earlier humorous period and remains rather superficial. Orchestrated for the music-hall, these four memories of his café-concert period in Montmartre ("Grande ritournelle," "Marche franco-lunaire," "Valse du mystérieux baiser

1920

dans l'œil," "Cancan grand-mondain") are not exempt from a certain vulgarity, which was of course intentional.[10]

Of the "Quatre petites mélodies," it is noteworthy that the "Elégie," a sober lament with a sorrowful and irregular melodic line, was dedicated to Claude Debussy, "in memory of an admiring and tender friendship of thirty years."[11] In the other three melodies, ("Danseuse," "Chanson," "Adieu"), Satie seems to give his music a more popular inflection. This tendency, present in "Chanson à boire," can be even more clearly identified in the five "Ludions," written for poems by Léon-Paul Fargue. This was one of Satie's most successful works, due to the perfect correlation between the inspiration of the poet and that of the musician. The familiar playfulness of Fargue's poems, their childish rhythms, their humorous nostalgia, are all delicately rendered by Satie. The lilting rhythm of "Air du rat," the ironical emphasis of "Spleen," the syncopations of "Grenouille américaine," the minor chords and the gentle monotony of "Air du poète," the liveliness of "Chanson du chat": all these small touches are achieved with such definitive precision that the irony shines through very clearly.

1923

"Mercure," three-dimensional poses in three images, is a short composition, made

**Mercure
1924**

[10] The "Premier menuet" (1920), for piano, is very vaguely reminiscent of the "Nocturnes." It is admirable for its classical and straightforward tone, as well as for its harmonious precision.

[11] Published in "Tombeau de Debussy," a special number of "Revue Musicale," 1920.

up of brilliant, lively scenes and full of charming fantasy which never becomes heavyhanded. It has been said that "Mercure" is the ballet of a great painter. It is true that Picasso used his great talents in the sets for "Mercure" and in its adorably deformed costumes. A painter of genius was having fun, along with his collaborators: Massine, who had imagined a lively and brutal choreography and who personified a leaping Mercury, and Satie.

The work was simple and clear, with no intent other than to spring things of beauty unexpectedly from their hiding-place beneath its jokes. The authors did not intend to create a mythological work; as Satie himself explained to a newspaperman:

These are simply antic persons, and the music is naturally country-fair music . . . . I believe that the music will convey fairly accurately what we have wanted to express. I have wanted it to be different from music-hall harmonies and to be composed of the very typical rhythms of itinerant actors (quoted in "Comœdia").

The orchestration further accentuated this country-fair atmosphere, giving a predominant role to brass instruments, especially the tuba, and thereby lending a certain vulgarity to the sonorities. This suite of thirteen brief pieces was not understood; the "emotional points of reference"[12] that Satie introduced in his score were missed. The misunderstanding came mainly from the eternal question of "genres"; people recognized certain sounds and rhythms which they associated with café-concert

[12] Paul Collaer.

music, and looked no further . . . . To certain musicians the music-hall appears synon-
ymous with vulgarity and poverty. To
gain critical approval, one must transpose
the simple rhythms in which one finds inspiration, giving them a certain distinc-
tion—artificial, to be sure. A duchess dressed
as a poor sewing girl does not feel at ease
except when she is unobserved. Have we
not witnessed innumerable instances of such
hybrid ballets, in which pavanes à la Ravel
are linked in contrived fashion to some lively
charleston? Thus is Art ravaged. The pieces
that Bach or Rameau based on gigue or
bourrée rhythms were certainly not "trans-
posed." M. Marnold says that the art of
music has been able to use these dances
"because they grew spontaneously out of a
movement of human joy, whereas the music-hall dances are essentially posturings
aimed at amusing the audience." The dis-
tinction, which appears fairly subtle, is not
the sort that Bach would have concerned
himself with—he simply adorned the popular rhythms he found around him with extremely beautiful themes, which he arranged
with his great proficiency in counterpoint.
In the same way, a study of the piano score
of "Mercure" reveals a great skill in composition.

After an overture in which two themes,
the one uneven and violent, the other singing (oboe), brilliantly overlap, the curtain
rises to a page of music in which all the
peacefulness of Satie's best work can be
found: "La Nuit." This is a sketch through
which the strings glide easily, while the

clarinet introduces mysterious effects. The
gentle "Danse de tendresse," a fugued waltz
on airy themes, achieves surprising grandeur. In "Signes du Zodiaque," which is
reminiscent of "Sports et divertissements,"
the tuba playfully presents a bright and gay
theme. The first part ends with the "very
singing" counterpoint of "Danse de Mercure."

The second part begins with the "Danse
des Grâces," a "distinguished" waltz, with
recurring phrases and notes which are
alternately legato and staccato. It changes
suddenly to the "Bain des Grâces," an unobtrusive, gently balanced string solo: pure
music in which beauty appears somehow
in a small, four-voice choral which is dis-
concertingly "naked." The brutal and syncopated "Fuite de Mercure" and "Colère
de Cerbère" break the spell and introduce
vivid colors.

The third part marks the triumph of
Satie's technique. In the "Polka des lettres,"
which can be compared to the "Danses" in
"Piège de Méduse," the trumpet comically
introduces a popular tune. This is followed
by "Nouvelle danse," which reveals the mysterious beauty of simple progressions of
chords; here the violas and later the violins
repeat a quiet, lightly chromatic melody with
an exquisite cadence. The polka resumes and
we have "Chaos," represented musically by
the "grandiose" superposition of the two
preceding themes: the woodwinds and brass
instruments play the "Polka des lettres,"
while the strings in unison, very legato, in-
tone the "Nouvelle danse." "Mercure" ends

on a very lively and brilliant finale. The last measures are forcefully repeated, already foreshadowing "Relâche."

Picabia's frontispiece for the score depicts a bearded gentleman, bald and seated on a cloud, who apparently is receiving advice from a sexless creature wearing only top hat and wristwatch. The legend explains the meaning of the allegory as well as the story of "Relâche": "When will people dehabituate themselves from the habit of explaining everything?" "Relâche" is "instantanéiste" ballet, aimed at the "pretentious absurdities" of the theater: "life as I love it, life without tomorrow, the life of today, everything for today, nothing for yesterday, nothing for tomorrow."[13] That is all very well, but one must not substitute one slogan for another, which is what Picabia and his accomplices did. (One exception of course is René Clair, whose film is a landmark in cinematography.) At least Picabia was enjoying himself, but was he not the only one who did? Perhaps Satie shared his fun; but for once he made a mistake. "Down with all academicisms" was certainly a slogan which must have pleased him enormously.

One should not be surprised if the score is not as solid as Satie's other works. "M. Satie's music consists of tired popular tunes, creating with relatively little effort a rather pure example of the low-class dance-hall genre." These are the words of Paul Souday, one of the most lenient of critics, who thus

Relâche

I want to compose a piece for dogs, and I already have my decor. The curtain rises on a bone.
Erik Satie
(quoted by Cocteau)

1924

[13] See the program of the Swedish Ballet, 1924.

expressed more or less Satie's own feelings. Satie had realized that the popular themes would be criticized; yet, given the libretto he had to work with, any other music would certainly have been ridiculous. But what does that matter, since he used these themes so skillfully? One need only read the piano score to notice that "Relâche" contains both a great wealth of expression and a great sense of fantasy; these are just as well developed as in Satie's other compositions. Certain rehearsals already testified that he must have felt uncomfortable in putting such a libretto to music. But if one looks at the various pieces ("Entrée de la femme," "Musique," "Entrée des hommes," "Les hommes se dévêtissent," "Danse de la brouette") one at a time, one will find real artistry, realized in light nuances and not in the least pedantic. The orchestration is intentionally clear and simple; the more gentle pages are supported by the strings and woodwinds, while the refrains are nimbly presented by the trumpets. Here and there one can find a few instrumental innovations, such as the dialogues between wind instruments which in "Les hommes se dévêtissent" "pleasantly" distort the popular "Cadet-Roussel." Over and above all this, and despite the clash of rhythms and of melodies in the music, a sort of unity pervades the entire composition. One may wonder whether Satie did not in fact wish to write "popular" music which could please both the simple people and the more sophisticated. Unfortunately, it pleased neither; the former because they were not invited to hear it, the latter because they declined to go.

Satie's score for "Entr'acte cinématographique" must be given special attention, not only in the context of the rest of Satie's works but also of the field of musical accompaniment of films. This was a field which Satie understood well, for he had a clear awareness of what such music should be. It should underscore the cinematic imagery and motion without taking on any importance in itself, without imposing itself through themes or chords that might divert the attention of the audience from the film. Its role must be purely decorative. It is therefore truly the extension of the principle of "musique d'ameublement." It is through repetitiveness that Satie decided to attain his aim. In his book "La Sensibilité Musicale" Landry mentions Kipling's little Hindu boy who casts a spell over his evenings by endlessly repeating a rhythmic figure on his drum. The pleasure comes from a semihypnotic state, conducive to dreams which are not created by the drum but for which the drum is a simple accompaniment. "In such cases," Landry adds, "the role of the musical element is accessory, analogous to the role it plays for instance in the cinema during the showing of a film." In "Entr'acte," measures composed of rhythmic and harmonic elements alone are repeated several times, whereas the melody remains secondary. Each of the fragments created in this way forms in a sense a cell with its own clearly defined tonality. These cells are attached to each other, often directly, without modulations, at times by way of a few measures that may be a little more singing in appeal. Each is different from all the others, except for one that reappears periodically throughout the score.[14] Gentle, melodic themes bring a restful note to the powerful dynamism of the whole ("La danseuse"). The middle part, accompanying the grotesque funeral procession, has real grandeur: it includes a funeral march with the theme played by a French horn, a slow processional, with rhythmic support by a rattle, which gradually accelerates until it culminates in "La poursuite," one of the most powerful musical evocations of speed. Following a sober choral, the music becomes more and more mechanical; to uniform percussion, it ascends the musical scale, modulating rapidly between widely-spaced notes. Finally, the music becomes calm and light, as the characters exit under Jean Borlin's baton.

[14] This technique of Satie's had been anticipated in a part of Milhaud's "Protée."

63

64
65

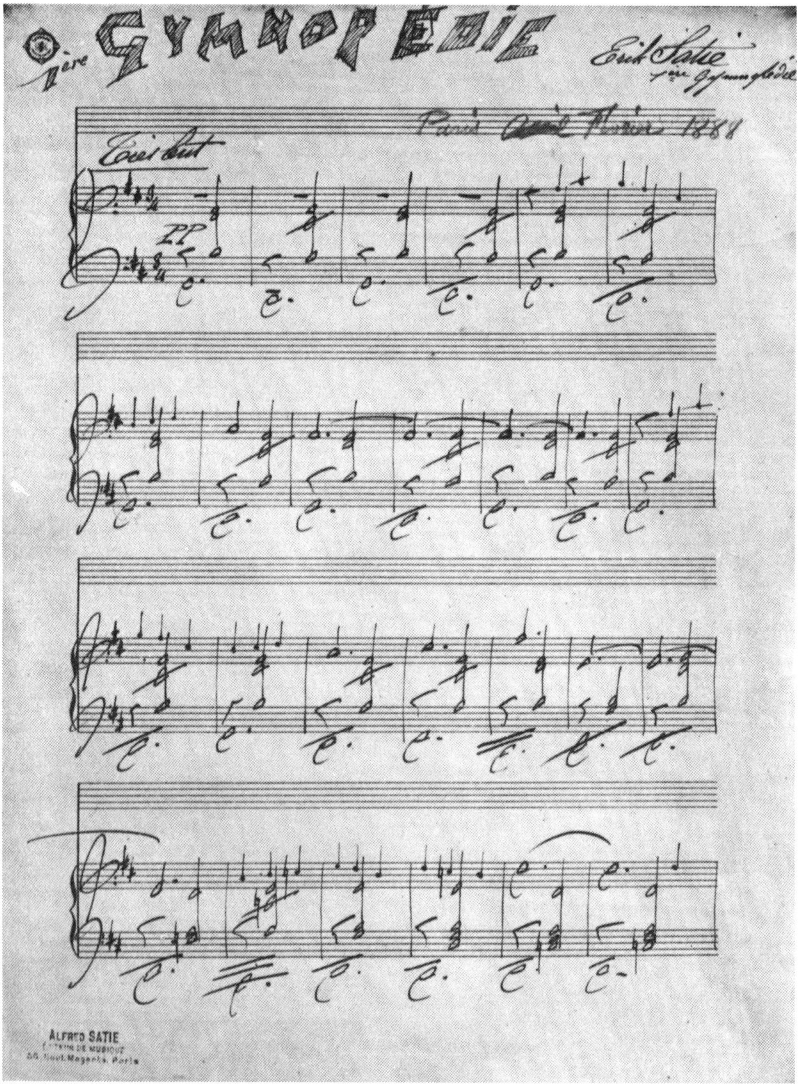

SENTIMENTS RELIGIEUX.

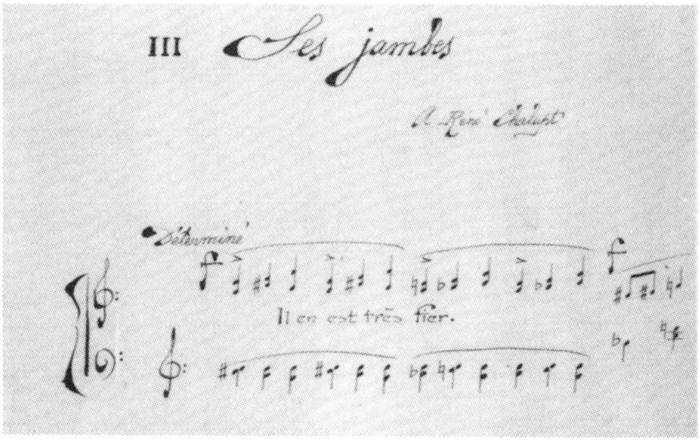
III Ses jambes
Déterminé
Il en est très fier.

Dis-moi, Daphénéo,
Ah!

Dis-moi
arbre dont les
1 bis
2 bis
3
4
5
6
C'est arbre
est un

Je ne ferai pas un cours de technologie
musicale, réduisant cette causerie à l'examen de l'Esprit musical —
proprement, Bref sujet déjà assez vaste spacieux, par lui-même.

Éviter d'entrer trop avant dans la technique pure —
ce qui serait un champs trop vaste, ici — mais parler de l'Esprit musical
La sagesse, l'abnégation, le sacrifice de Soi-même.
La lutte
La question "métier"
Être "doué" (ce que c'est ?)
Le courage
La patience. Arrivé ?.... arrivé à quoi ?
Les grands Musiciens (citer Debussy, Liszt, César Franck)
Wagner (son influence n'existe plus, pour la jeunesse actuelle)
Le contrepoint (son esprit). Les contrapontistes)Mle
L'Harmonie (son esprit).
La Mélodie (son esprit) L'imagination
Le Rythme (son esprit)
La Sonorité (son esprit) Ignorance
Le Dynamisme (son esprit) L'esprit dynamique
L'Esprit tonal (Question d'équilibre)
L'Esprit Atonal (Saint-Saens & certains compositeurs.
Chopin, Schumann). Son apport dans la Musique moderne.
Le sens Créateur.

Il faut tout cela pour constituer un musicien, un
artiste (mot que je n'aime pas beaucoup).

confesser à la fin ce qu'il veu cachera d'abord.

G Valère :
Voilà une étrange folie !

Martine :
Il est vrai ; mais après cela, vous verrez qu'il fait des merveilles.

Valère :
Comment s'appelle-t-il ?

Martine :
Il s'appelle Sganarelle.

Lucas :
Tétigué ! v'là justement l'homme

75
76

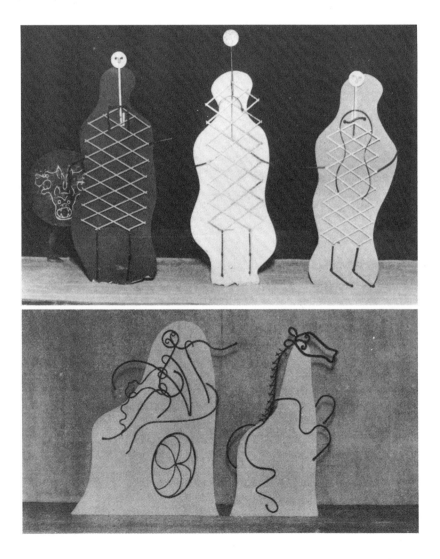

7
8
9
10
11
12
13
LA majeur (Andante)
Elégant (début)
Bal
Polka des lettres (16 mesures) — Fa maj.
Nouvelles Danses (16 mesures — La maj.
Apparition du Char (les deux précédentes l'une sur l'autre) — UT maj.
64 × 8 — Fa maj.
Rapt de Proserpine (FINAL)
etc.
20

82 83

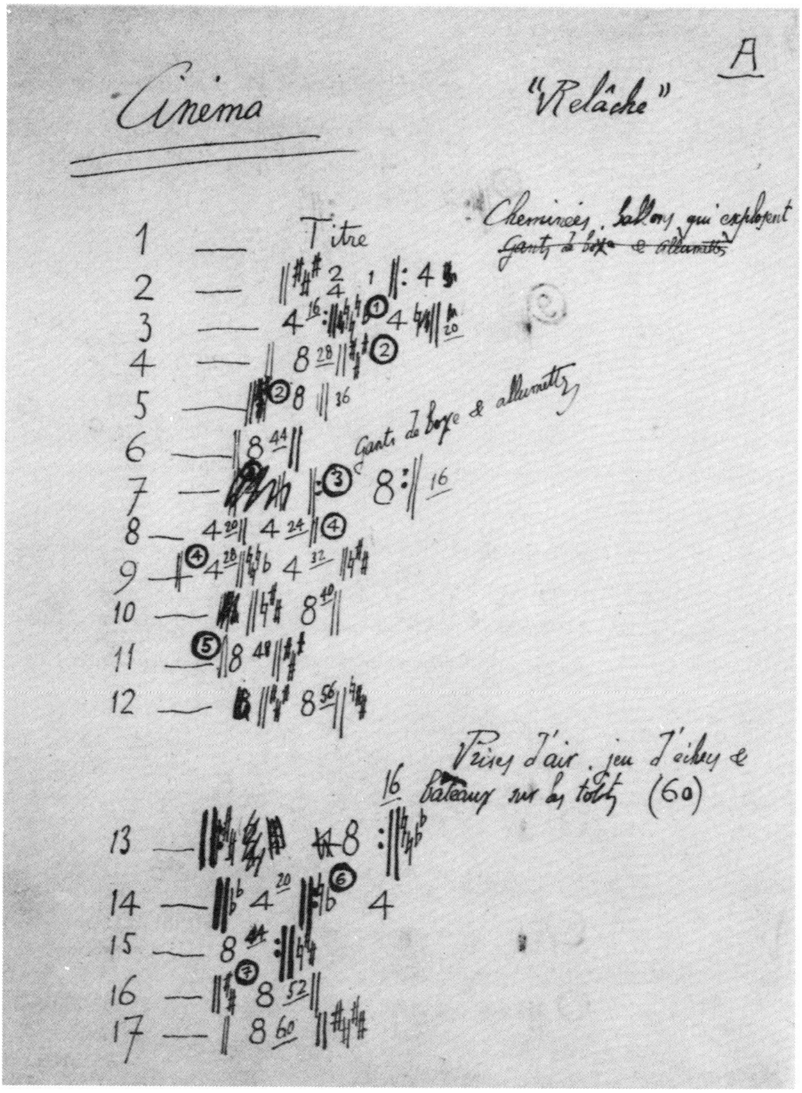
A
Cinema
"Relâche"
Cheminées, ballons qui explosent
Titre
Gants de boxe & allumettes
Prises d'air, jeu d'échecs & bateaux sur les toits (60)

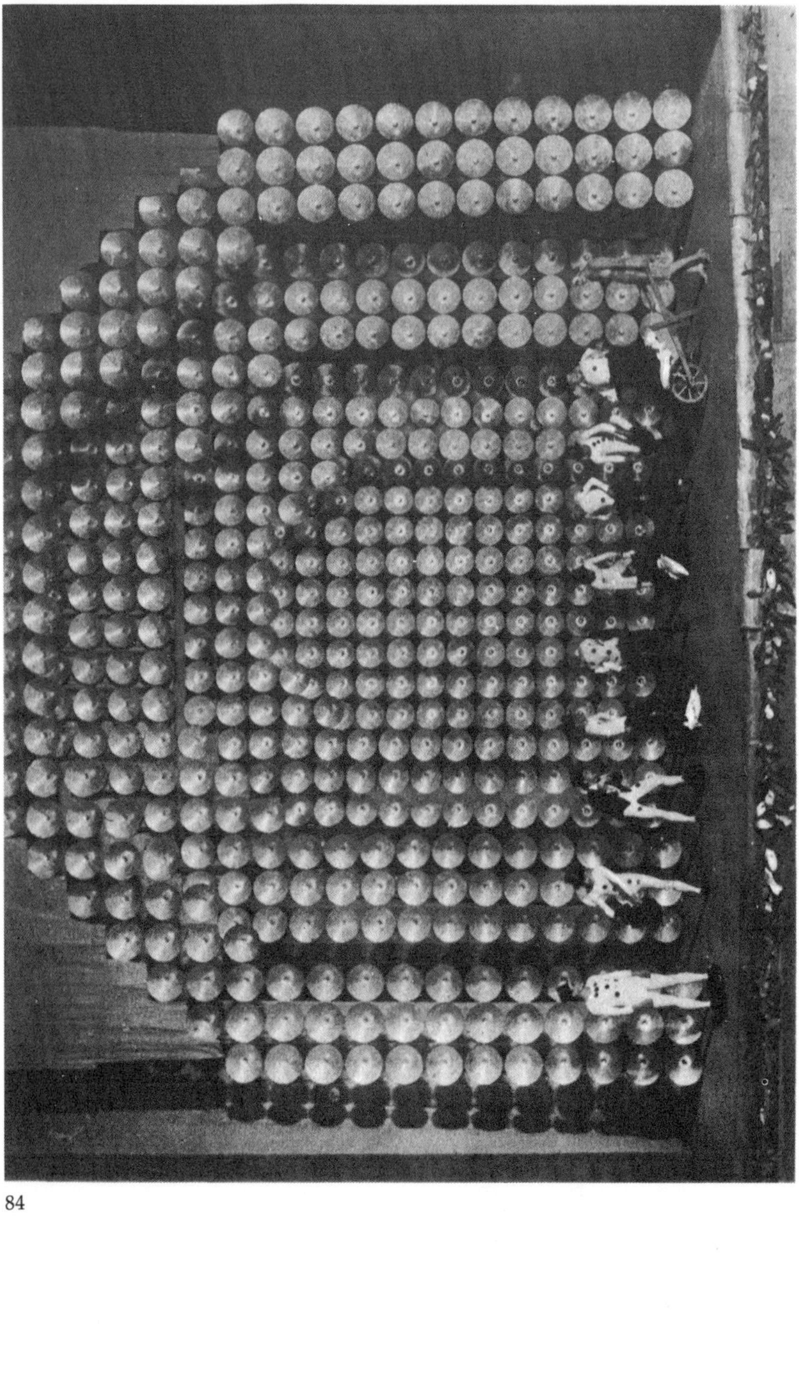

4

En Plus

This small volume has only one pretension:
to be sincere. We have tried here to remain
as far removed from "literature" as from
snobbism. Both have hurt Satie considerably; and Boris de Schloezer was not entirely
wrong when he wrote in 1924 that "the
Satie case" belonged more properly to the
realm of literary than to that of musical criti-
cism. Today his name no longer appears
on concert programs; and although we consider this to be an excellent thing, its con-
sequence is that we cannot "judge" him.
One should differentiate between judging
and appreciating; that is why we do not feel
that we are contradicting here the state-
ments made earlier in this brief study of
Satie's work. We have used the word beauty
in a completely personal sense. It is impossible to judge without first establishing a
code of values; to apply it, in turn, one must
resort to comparisons, points of reference.
Satie, however, is a unique phenomenon.

Some have called him the greatest musician of all time; his enemies, or the "pawns,"

as he called them in his deep voice, in turn called him a buffoon. Happily, he was neither. Commenting on "Relâche" in his "Etudes," Darius Milhaud speaks of the qualities "which give his work its character of authenticity and perfection." It is precisely "authenticity" that describes Satie's very delicate art and which will undoubtedly allow his compositions to survive, as it has done for the works of musicians—Couperin, for instance—who did not leave behind an "œuvre." On the other hand, authenticity cannot be proved; one can only invoke, as we have done in this book, the evidence and the compromises which suggest it.

There is also his exemplary life, the thirty years of solitary meditation, his great integrity and his modesty, and his submissiveness to music, all of which made of Satie a rare and pure figure.

He is unknown. Many critics were long ago antagonized by his witty titles and eccentricity; and they negated his music without knowing it. In an obituary, one of "those gentlemen" described the gentle "Gymnopédies" as humorous pieces. Others claimed that Satie, ignorant of the fundamentals of music, had as a shrewd Norman exploited the rich possibilities of humor to mask his technical inadequacies. We must not forget that Satie was certainly the most insulted of musicians during the whole of his long artistic existence. He was obliged to develop great courage in the face of this systematic malevolence and the sneers directed at him. His evident talent was despised, his sincerity questioned, his intentions misinterpreted; he was constantly criticized for his ignorance, his dilettantism. Only foreign musicians did not levy these charges against him, because they judged him by his works alone:

As for the nightingale, so often mentioned, its musical knowledge makes even the most ignorant listener shrug his shoulders. Not only is its voice not properly 'placed'; it is completely ignorant on the subject of key, tonality, modality, and time. Could it be that the nightingale has talent? This is possible, even certain. But it can be stated that its artistic culture lags behind its natural gifts, and that this voice of which it is so proud is only a very inferior instrument, having no value in itself. (Erik Satie, "Intelligence and Musical Appreciation among Animals").

Posterity is not infallible; will it retain the name of this musician, this disinterested innovator? Will it allow the fine and profound notations of this explorer who had "glimpsed a new world" to fall into oblivion? It would be a loss for those—and they will surely always exist, despite the seductive rapture of sound—who love to keep by them a "bedside music" which is smiling without affectation, deep without insistence, and which appeases without boring.

Erik Satie:
A Discography

The following is a list of (substantially) all recordings of Satie's music issued, both foreign and domestic. However, many of these records are withdrawn or unobtainable; consult a current listing, such as the Schwann catalog, for items readily available.

Aperçus désagréables (1908) Pf., 4 hds.
A. Ciccolini.[1] Angel (s)S-36459; Col.(F) FCX 1.046, (s)SAXF 1.046, (s)CVC 1046.

Avant-dernières pensées (1915) Pf. solo
H. Boschi. MF program 623.
A. Ciccolini. Angel 35442; Col.(F) FCX 561.
A. Ciccolini. Angel (s)S-36482; Col.(F) FCX 998, (s)SAXF 998, (s)CVC 998; HMV (s)ASD 2389.
E. Crochet. Phi. (s)PHS900–179.
J. Fevrier. Everest (s)3221; Adès (s)7023/24.
F. Glazer. Vox (s)SVBX 5422.
F. Poulenc. Col. ML 4399; BAM LD 023.

La Belle excentrique (1920) Music-hall orch.
. . . Grand Ritournelle.
Utah sym. orch.; M. Abravanel, cond. Van. (s)VCS 10037/38.
Version for Pf., 4 hds. (1920)
A. Ciccolini.[1] Angel (s)S-36459; Col.(F) FCX 1.046, (s)SAXF 1.046, (s)CVC 1046; HMV (s)ASD 2389.
J. Fevrier. F. Poulenc. Fid. (s)34.002.

Chapitres tournés en tous sens (1913) Pf. solo
A. Ciccolini. Angel (s)S-36459; Col.(F) FCX 1.046, (s)SAXF 1.046, (s)CVC 1046.

F. Glazer. Vox (s)SVBX 5422.
W. Masselos. MGM E3154.

**Croquis et agaceries d'un gros bonhomme en
bois** (1. Tyrolienne turque. 2. Danse maigre.
3. Españaña) (1913) Pf. solo
A. Ciccolini. Col.(F) *16.020.
A. Ciccolini. Angel (s)S-36482; Col.(E) FCX 998,
(s)SAXF 998, (s)CVC 998.
J. Fevrier. Everest (s)3221, Adès (s)7023/24.
F. Glazer. Vox (s)SVBX 5422.
F. Poulenc. Col. ML 4399. (Nos. 1 & 2 only:
BAM LD023)

Danses gothiques (1893) Pf. solo
F. Glazer. Vox (s)SVBX 5422.

Descriptions automatiques (1913) Pf. solo
A. Ciccolini. Angel (s)S-36459; Col. (F) FCX 1.046,
(s)SAXF 1.046, (s)CVC 1046; HMV (s)ASD 2389.
F. Glazer. Vox (s)SVBX 5422.
F. Poulenc. Col. ML 4399; BAM LD023.
J. Wiener.[2] MF program 160.

Désespoir agréable Pf. solo
E. Crochet. Phi. (s)PHS 900–179.

(La) Diva de l'empire. Voice and pf.
"Colinette," Sop. and pf. CDM #PM1606, LDA
4003.
. . . arr. pf. H. Ourdine.
W. Masselos. MGM E3154.

Effronterie. Pf. solo.
E. Crochet. Phi. (s)PHS900–179.

Embryons desséchés (1913) Pf. solo
A. Ciccolini. Angel (s)S-36485; Col.(F) (s)CVC
1104; HMV (s)ASD 2389.
J. Fevrier. Everest (s)3221, Adès (s)7023/24.
F. Glazer. Vox (s)SVBX 5422.
W. Masselos. MGM E3154.

Enfantillages pittoresques (1913) Pf. solo
A. Ciccolini. Angel (s)S-36485; Col.(F) (s)CVC
1104.
F. Glazer. Vox (s)SVBX 5422.
M. Richter. MGM E3181.

(Le) Fils des étoiles. (3) Preludes (1891) Pf. solo
. . . No. 1.
J. Barbier. BAM LD093, (s)5.093.
. . . orch. Roland-Manuel.

Utah sym. orch.; M. Abravanel, cond. Van.
(s)VCS 10037/38.

(6) Gnossiennes (1890) Pf. solo
E. Crochet. Phi. (s)PHS 900–179.
. . . Nos. 1–3.
J. Barbier. BAM LD093, (s)5.093.
A. Bernot. SFP 30C2M.
H. Boschi. CDM LDA 4003.
A. Ciccolini. Angel 35442; Col.(F) FCX 561, *16.020.
A. Ciccolini. Angel (s)S-36482; Col.(F) FCX 998,
(s)SAXF 998, (s)CVC 998; HMV (s)ASD 2389.
F. Glazer. Vox (s)SVBX 5422.
W. Masselos. MGM E3154.
. . . No. 1 only.
G. Copeland. Vic. #1629; Vic.(J) #JF 33.
J. Fevrier. Everest (s)3221, Adès (s)7023/24.
. . . No. 2 only.
L. Thyrion. Phi. (E) N00601R.
. . . No. 3 only.
G. Casadesus. Vox #16005 (Set #163).
F. Poulenc. Col. ML 4399; BAM LD023.
. . . No. 3 orch. F. Poulenc.[3]
Utah sym. orch.; M. Abravanel, cond. Van.
(s)VCS 10037/38.

(La) Grenouille du jeu de tonneau. Voice and pf.
D. Benoit, sop., J. Wiener, pf. MF program 485–86.

(5) Grimaces pour "Un Songe d'une Nuit d'Eté"
(1914) Orch.
Utah sym. orch.; M. Abravanel, cond. Van.
(s)VCS 10037/38.

(3) Gymnopédies (1888) Pf. solo
J. Barbier. BAM LD093, (s)5.093.
A. Bernot. SFP 30C2M.
A. Ciccolini. PM *17.055.
A. Ciccolini. Angel (s)S-36482; Col.(F) FCX 998,
(s)SAXF 998, (s)CVC 998; HMV (s)ASD 2389.
E. Crochet. Phi. (s)PHS900–179.
F. Glazer. Vox (s)SVBX 5422.
W. Masselos. MGM E3154.
D. Merlet. MF program 520.
. . . No. 1 only.
J. Fevrier. Everest (s)3221, Adès (s)7023/24.
F. Poulenc. Col. ML 4399; BAM LD023.
J. Wiener. MF program 160.
. . . No. 3 only.
G. Copeland. MGM E151, E3024.

P. Gordon. MF program 215.

M. Pressler. MGM E3129.

. . . Arr. orch. (nos. 1, 3, C. Debussy[4]; no. 2, R. Jones).

Concert arts orch.; V. Golschmann, cond. Cap. P 8244; Cap.(D) CTL 7055.

. . . . Nos. 1 and 3 only.

Boston sym. orch.; S. Koussevitzky, cond. Vic. LM-2651, SP33–181; Cam. CAL 376; Vic.(E) RB 6533; Gr. *7RF 185; Vic. *49–0771, *ERA 195, #12–1060; Vic.(F) *A95208.

Concert arts orch.; V. Golschmann, cond. Cap. *FAP 8252.

Hague phil. orch.; W. Otterloo, cond. Phi.(E) SBR 6234, *SBF242.

London sym. orch.; A. Previn, cond. Vic. LM 2945, (s)LSC 2945; Vic.(E) RB 6721, (s)SB 6721; Vic.(F)(s) 645.082.

Paris chamber orch.; C. Brück, cond. MF program 520.

Paris Conservatoire orch.; L. Auriacombe, cond. Angel (s)S-36486; HMV (s)ASD 2369; Col.(F) (s)CVC 2034.

Philadelphia orch.; L. Stokowski, cond. Vic. #1965.

Utah sym. orch.; M. Abravanel, cond. Van. (s)VCS 10037/38

. . . No. 1 only. Arr. harmonica and orch. Garden, har.; orch. cond. F. Rauber. Phi.(E) G 05.578R, (s)836.393V2.

. . . Arr. harp and orch. L. Challen, harp. Col. (F)(s) CCA 1.102

. . . No. 3 only.

Boston sym. orch.; S. Koussevitzky, cond. Vic. #7252 (set #M-352); Gr. #D 1860, #AW 176.

. . . Arr. 2 pfs.

. . . No. 2 only.

A. Whittemore, J. Lowe. Vic. LM-1926.

En Habit de cheval (1911) Orch.

Utah sym. orch.; M. Abravanel, cond. Van. (s)VCS 10037/38.

Orchestre national de l'Office de Radiodiffusion-Télévision Française; M. Rosenthal, cond. Adès (s)7023/24.

. . Version for pf., 4 hds. (1911).

A. Ciccolini.[1] Angel (s)S-36459; Col.(F) FCX 1.046, (s)SAXF 1.046, (s)CVC 1.046.

A. Gold, R. Fizdale. Col. ML 4854 (set SL-198).
J. Fevrier. F. Poulenc. Fid. (s)34.002.

Heures séculaires et instantanées (1914) Pf. solo
A. Ciccolini. Angel 35442; Col.(F) FCX 561.
A. Ciccolini. Angel (s)S-36482; Col.(F) FCX 998,
(s)SAXF 998, (s)CVC 998.
F. Glazer. Vox (s)SVBX 5422.

Jack-in-the-Box (1899) Pf. solo
. . . . orch. D. Milhaud (1929).
Utah sym. orch.; M. Abravanel, cond. Van.
(s)VCS 10037/38.

Je te veux (valse) (1900?) Small orch.
Orch. cond. Chevreux. CDM LDYM 4020.
. . Version for voice and pf.
A. Capri., sop. with pf. CDM #2001.
"Colinette", sop. and pf. CDM LDA4003.
J. Tourel, mezzo-sop., G. Reeves, pf. Col. ML 4158.
. . . . arr. pf.
J. Wiener. Col.(F) #D15005.

Ludions (1923) Voice and pf.
A. Laloë, sop., J. Wiener, pf. MF program 160.
. . . Selections.
D. Benoît, sop., J. Wiener, pf. MF program 485–86.

(3) Mélodies (1. La Statue de Bronze. 2. Daphé-
néo. 3. Le Chapelier) (1916) Voice and pf.
J. Bathori, sop., D. Milhaud, pf. VI 50.030; Col.
#9132M; Col.(E) #D15195; Col.(J) #SW 276.
P. Bernac, bar., F. Poulenc, pf. Col. ML 4484;
Ody. 32260009.
C. Castelli, sop., H. Boschi, pf. CDM LDA4003.
. . . Nos. 1 and 3.
P. Bernac, bar., F. Poulenc, pf. Gr. #DA 4893.
. . . No. 3 only.
J. Tourel, mezzo-sop., G. Reeves, pf. Col. ML 4158.

Menuet (1920) Pf. solo.
F. Glazer. Vox (s)SVBX 5422.

Menus propos enfantins (1913) Pf. solo.
A. Ciccolini. Angel (s)S-36485; Col.(F) (s)CVC
1104.
F. Glazer. Vox (s)SVBX 5422.
M. Richter. MGM E3181.

Mercure (1924). Ballet.
Utah sym. orch.; M. Abravanel, cond. Van.
(s)VCS 10037/38.

Messe pour les pauvres (1895) Organ or pf.

M. Mason, organ; chorus cond. D. Randolph.
Count.-Eso. 507, MC 20013, (s)5507.

(3) Morceaux en forme de poire (1903) Pf. 4 hds.
G. Auric, J. Fevrier. Everest (s)3221; Adès (s)
7023/24.
H. Boschi, S. Nigg. CDM LDA4003.
R. and G. Casadesus. Col. ML 4246, #17545/47D
(set #MM 763).
R. and G. Casadesus. Col. ML 5723, (s)MS 6323;
Col.(F) 72.050.
A. Ciccolini.[1] Angel 35442; Col.(F) FCX 561.
A. Ciccolini.[1] Angel (s)S-36482; Col.(F) FCX 998,
(s)SAXF 998, (s)CVC 998; HMV (s)ASD 2389.
. . . Nos. 1, 2.
J. Fevrier, F. Poulenc. Fid. (s)34.002.
G. Auric, F. Poulenc. BAM #17.
. . . orch. R. Desormière.
Utah sym. orch.; M. Abravanel, cond. Van.
(s)VCS 10037/38.

(5) Nocturnes (1919) Pf. solo
A. Bernot. SFP 30C2M.
F. Glazer. Vox (s)SVBX 5422.
J. Wiener. MF program 485–86.
. . . Nos. 1–3.
A. Ciccolini. Angel 35442; Col.(F) FCX 561.
A. Ciccolini. Angel (s)S-36482; Col.(F) FCX 998,
(s)SAXF 998, (s)CVC 998.
. . No. 3 only.
L. Thyrion. Phi.(E) N00601R.
. . . No. 4 only.
J. Wiener. MF program 160.
. . . No. 5 only.
W. Masselos. MGM E3154.

Nouvelles pièces froides. Pf. solo
E. Crochet. Phi. (s)PHS900–179.

(4) Ogives (1886) Pf. solo
F. Glazer. Vox (s)SVBX 5422.
. . . Nos. 1 and 4.
J. Barbier. BAM LD093, (s)5.093.

(Les) pantins dansent (1914) Pf. solo
A. Ciccolini. Angel (s)S-36485; Col.(F) (s)CVC
1104.
F. Glazer. Vox (s)SVBX 5422.

Parade (1917) Ballet realiste.
Houston sym. orch.; E. Kurtz, cond. Col. ML 2112,
#MM 913.

London sym. orch.; A. Dorati, cond. Mer. 50435,
(s)90435; Phi.(E) (s)SAL 3637.
Orchestre national de l'Opéra de Monte Carlo;
L. Frémaux, cond. DGG LPM 18649, (s)SLPM
138649.
Paris Conservatoire orch.; L. Auriacombe, cond.
Angel (s)S-36486; HMV (s)ASD 2369; Col.(F)
(s)CVC 2034.
Orchestre national de l'Office de Radiodiffusion-
Télévision Française; M. Rosenthal, cond. Adès
(s)7023/24.
Philharmonia orch.; I. Markevitch, cond. Angel
35151 (set 3518C); Col.(E) 33CX 1197, FCX 357.
Utah sym. orch.; M. Abravanel, cond. Van.
(s)VCS 10037/38.
. . . Suite, pf. 4-hds. (1917).
G. Auric, F. Poulenc. BAM #16/17.

Passacaille (1906) Pf. solo
A. Ciccolini. Angel (s)S-36485; Col.(F) (s)CVC
1104; HMV (s)ASD 2389.
F. Glazer. Vox (s)SVBX 5422.

Peccadilles importunes (1913) Pf. solo
A. Ciccolini. Angel (s)S-36485; Col.(F) (s)CVC
1104.
F. Glazer. Vox (s)SVBX 5422.
M. Richter. MGM E3181.

Petite ouverture à danser. Pf. solo
E. Crochet. Phi. (s)PHS900–179.

(3) Petites pièces montées (1919) Small orch.
Leningrad philh. chamb. orch.; G. Rozhdestven-
sky, cond. ME 74075KK.[5]
London chamb. orch.; A. Bernard, cond. Vic.
LM 6092–2; HMV HLP26.[6]
Sym. orch. cond. P. Chagnon. Col. #68887D;
Col.(E) #50292D, #D11016.
Orchestre national de l'Office de Radiodiffusion-
Télévision Française; M. Rosenthal, cond. Adès
(s)7023/24.
. . . Version for pf. (1921).
. . . . No. 1 only. De l'Enfance de Pantagruel
(Rêverie).
A. Ciccolini. Angel (s)S-36485; Col.(F) (s)CVC
1104.
F. Glazer. Vox (s)SVBX 5422.

Pièces froides (1. (3) Airs à faire fuir. 2. (3)
Danses de travers.) (1897) Pf. solo

A. Bernot. SFP 30C2M.
A. Ciccolini. Angel (s)S-36485; Col.(F) (s)CVC
1104.
F. Glazer. Vox (s)SVBX 5422.
. . . . No. 1 only.
J. Barbier. BAM LD093, (s)5.093.
. . . . No. 2 only.
H. Boschi. MF program 624.
. . . . Air no. 1; Danse no. 1.
J. Fevrier. Everest (s)3221, Adès (s)7023/24.

(Le) Piège de Méduse (1913) Comedy with music.
Chamber group
. . . . Selections, arr. pf. 4 hds. (1920).
A. Ciccolini. Angel (s)S-36485; Col.(F) (s)CVC
1104; HMV (s)ASD 2389.

(3) Poèmes d'amour (1914) Voice and pf.
A. Loloë, sop., J. Wiener, pf. MF program 160.

Prélude canin. Pf. solo
E. Crochet. Phi. (s)PHS900–179.

Prélude de la porte héroïque du ciel (1894) Pf.
solo
F. Glazer. Vox (s)SVBX 5422.
F. Poulenc. BAM LD023.

Prélude en tapisserie (1906) Pf. solo
A. Ciccolini. Angel (s)S-36485; Col.(F) (s)CVC
1104.
F. Glazer. Vox (s)SVBX 5422.

(4) Préludes (1. Fête en l'honneur d'une jeune
demoiselle. 2. Prélude d'Eginhard. 3. 1ère Pré-
lude du Nazaréen. 4. 2me Prélude du Nazaréen)
(1893) Pf. solo
F. Glazer. Vox (s)SVBX 5422.
. . . No. 1 only.
C. Martin. Educo 5008.
F. Poulenc. BAM LD023.
. . . Nos. 1, 3 orch. Poulenc.[3]
Utah sym. orch.; M. Abravanel, cond. Van.
(s)VCS10037/38.

Préludes flasques (pour un chien) (1912) Pf. solo
A. Ciccolini. Angel (s)S-36485; Col.(F) (s)CVC
1104; HMV (s)ASD 2389.

Première pensée Rose-Croix. Pf. solo
E. Crochet. Phi. (s)PHS900–179.

Profondeur. Pf. solo
E. Crochet. Phi. (s)PHS900–179.

Relâche (1924). Ballet instantanéiste.
Paris Conservatoire orch.; L. Auriacombe, cond.
Angel (s)S-36486; HMV (s)ASD 2369; Col.(F)
(s)CVC 2034.
Utah sym. orch.; M. Abravanel, cond. Van.
(s)VCS 10037/38.

(2) Rêveries nocturnes. Pf. solo
E. Crochet. Phi. (s)PHS900–179.

(3) Sarabandes (1887) Pf. solo
A. Ciccolini. Angel (s)S-36485; Col.(F) (s)CVC
1104.
F. Glazer. Vox (s)SVBX 5422.
. . . No. 1 only.
J. Fevrier. Everest (s)3221, Adès (s)7023/24.
. . . . No. 2 only.
F. Poulenc. Col. ML 4399; BAM LD023.

Socrate (1919). Drame symphonique.
G. Friedmann, J. Giradeau, tens.; J. Jansen,
B. Demigny, bars.; French broadcasting system
chamb. orch.; C. Brück, cond. MF program
485–86.
V. Journeaux, J. Lindenfelder, S. Pèbordes,
A. Carpenter, sops.; French radio sym.; R. Leibo-
witz, cond. Count.-Eso. 510, MC 20006, (s)5510.
A. Laloë, sop.; orch. cond. Sauget. CDM LDX-A
8.292.
. . . Part 3 only. Le mort de Socrate. D. Monteil,
sop.; Orchestre national de l'Office de Radio-
diffusion-Télévision Française; M. Rosenthal,
cond. Adès (s)7023/24.
. . . Part 3 only. Arr. voice and pf.
P. Derenne, ten.; H. Sauget, pf. Pac. ES 1023;
Orphée 51.023

Sonatine bureaucratique (1917) Pf. solo
F. Glazer. Vox (s)SVBX 5422.
O. Penna. Odeon (A) #66051.

Songe-creux. Pf. solo
E. Crochet. Phi. (s)PHS900–179.

Sonneries de la Rose-Croix (1. Air de l'Ordre.
2. Air du grand Maître. 3. Air du grand Prieur)
(1892) Pf. solo
. . . Nos. 1 and 3.
J. Barbier. BAM LD093, (s)5.093.
. . . No. 2 only.
J. Wiener. MF program 160.

Sports et divertissements. (1914) Pf. solo
J. Barbier. BAM LD093, (s)5.093.
A. Ciccolini. Angel (s)S-36459; Col.(F) FCX 1.046,
(s)SAXF 1.046, (s)CVC 1046.
F. Glazer. Vox (s)SVBX 5422.
W. Masselos. MGM E3154.

Tendrement (1900?) Voice and pf.
"Colinette," sop. and pf. CDM LDA4003.

(3) Valses distinguées du précieux Dégoûté
(1914) Pf. solo
A. Ciccolini. Angel 35442; Col.(F) FCX 561.
A. Ciccolini. Angel (s)S-36482; Col.(F) FCX 998,
(s)SAXF 998, (s)CVC 998.
E. Crochet. Phi. (s)PHS900–179.
F. Glazer. Vox (s)SVBX 5422.

Véritables préludes flasques (pour un chien)
(1912) Pf. solo
A. Ciccolini. Angel (s)S-36459; Col.(F) FCX 1.046,
(s)SAXF 1.046, (s)CVC 1046; HMV (s)ASD 2389.
F. Glazer. Vox (s)SVBX 5422.
W. Masselos. MGM E3154.

Vieux séquins et vieilles cuirasses (1914) Pf. solo
A. Ciccolini. Angel (s)S-36459; Col.(F) FCX 1.046,
(s)SAXF 1.046, (s)CVC 1046.
F. Glazer. Vox (s)SVBX 5422.

(s) preceding a serial number indicates a stereo recording; # indicates a 78-r.p.m. recording; * indicates a 45-r.p.m. recording; all others are 33-1/3-r.p.m. (LP).

Symbols and Manufacturer Abbreviations

BAM Boîte à Musique.
Cam RCA Camden.
Cap. Capitol (US).
Cap. (D) Capitol (Decca-England).
CDM Chant du Monde.
Col. Columbia (US).
Col. (F) Columbia (France) (Pathé-Marconi).
Count.-Eso. Counterpoint-Esoteric.
DGG Deutsche Grammophon Gesellschaft.
Fid. Fidelio (UK)
Gr. Gramophone Co., Ltd. (UK).
HMV His Master's Voice (UK).
ME Melodiya Eurodise.
Mer. Mercury.

MF Masterworks from France. French Broadcasting System in North America (noncommercial).

Odeon (A) Odeon (Argentina).

Ody. Odyssey, Columbia (US).

Pac. Pacific (Marcuse) (Germany).

Phi. Philips (US).

Phi. (E) Philips (Europe).

PM Plaisir musical (Pathé).

SFP Société Française de Productions Phonographiques.

Van. Vanguard Cardinal.

VI Voix Illustres (Pathé).

Vic. RCA Victor (US).

Vic. (E) RCA Victor (UK).

Vic. (F) RCA Victor (France).

Vic. (J) RCA Victor (Japan).

Notes

1. Both parts performed by Ciccolini, by re-recording one part upon the other.
2. With simultaneous reading of Satie's inscriptions by A. Laloë.
3. Included under the title, "Deux préludes posthumes et une gnossienne."
4. Nos. 1 and 2 of the Debussy arrangements are nos. 3 and 1, respectively, of the original piano versions.
5. Labeled as "Trois pièces après Gargantua et Pantagruel."
6. The History of Music in Sound, Vol. X.